A DATE FOR DAISY

TARA GRACE ERICSON

SILVER FOUNTAIN PRESS

Paperback ISBN-13: 978-1-949896-12-1
Ebook ISBN-13: 978-1-949896-10-7

To my father,
who loves unconditionally,
like Jesus does.

He who was seated on the throne said, "I am making everything new!" Then he said, "Write this down, for these words are trustworthy and true."

— Revelation 21:5

CONTENTS

PROLOGUE

October on the farm was one of Laura Bloom's favorite times. The leaves on the trees near the creek were changing near the top, and the warm colors would slowly migrate toward the ground over the next few weeks. The harvest season was winding down, the busyness of summer retreating into the comfortable rhythm of shorter days.

Laura jotted down thoughts of gratitude and praise in the open journal on her lap, then sipped the coffee Keith brought to her a few minutes before. These peaceful moments, cozied under a blanket in the armchair tucked in the corner of their bedroom, were treasured. She'd started the routine when the children were young, waking before little feet padded down the hallway and entered her room.

It was a minor thing, a few moments before the business of the day to spend with her Creator in prayer, but it made all the difference. Seven children. She reserved each day of the week to pray for one of them specifically-their faith, dreams, health, and future spouse. On the bulletin board posted next to the chair, pictures of her family and hand-written scriptures were visual reminders of her prayer list.

Her gaze wandered over a picture, snapped on a whim three years ago before Andi went on her second deployment. It landed on Daisy, her prayer focus for today. Unbidden, a smile twitched on her face. Daisy was her temperamental artist; her head in the clouds most days. A free-spirit, Keith always said, and wildly different from her twin sister, Andi, who thrived on order and routine.

These days, Daisy was channeling her creative energy into the soon-to-be Bloom's Farm Bed and Breakfast. She came to brunch each Saturday brimming with excitement about all she had accomplished during the week.

Laura prayed for Daisy's future husband. She didn't know who it would be, or even if it would be, but a mother knew one thing: it would take a special man to capture the heart of her free-spirited daughter. Was there a man who could let Daisy fly while holding her close?

1

*D*aisy ran her hand over the polished wooden banister as she walked up the stairs. It had been foolish to clean it up before finishing other projects, but reviving the intricate woodwork had been irresistible. Her contractor, Greg, even complimented the job she'd done. As much as Daisy wanted to handle everything herself, her shotgun approach to renovation projects was admittedly not ideal.

This morning, Daisy moved her attention to the bedrooms upstairs. Once the baseboards were gone, they could sand the hardwood floors and refinish them. She tugged gently on the baseboards, trying to preserve the original woodwork. The board broke free, and Daisy set it aside.

Greg planned to get here later today and Daisy checked her watch while she grabbed a protein bar, her usual lunch. Since she hired Greg, they'd knocked down walls and stripped the flooring downstairs. The progress was still slow, but Daisy kept costs low and tried to learn as much as she could. The retired contractor was patient and good-natured, happy to dig into the project with her and fill a few days a week.

The room was dim, despite the window, and Daisy studied the ceiling. An unfortunate reality of the old house was the lack of overhead lights. She'd have to run wiring for new lights in the attic. Where was Greg? She checked her watched again, then heard buzzing from across the room. Her phone flashed from its resting place in the corner and she crawled over to it.

"Hey, Greg."

"Miss Bloom, good morning." Greg always called her Miss Bloom, no matter how many times she invited him to call her Daisy.

Daisy laughed, "It's not morning anymore. It's nearly one-thirty. Are you still coming today? I've got some ideas for the bedrooms upstairs I want to run past you."

"Well, that's actually why I'm calling. You know

I've been having some trouble with my knees?" His groans and slow movement were evidence that he'd been struggling with the constant up and down of the renovation. Daisy's heart sank when Greg continued, "I went to the doctor this morning and they told me the cartilage is almost completely gone. They are recommending a replacement."

"Like a knee replacement?" Even though she knew the answer, Daisy needed to hear him say it.

"Yeah." Greg sighed before continuing. "They scheduled it for next week but told me not to aggravate it further. Which means no projects for me—at least not for a while."

Daisy laid herself on the old wood floor, staring at the ceiling. Selfishly, disappointment filled her as the implications for her bed-and-breakfast seeped into her thoughts. Greg had become a friend, and it would kill him to back out of the project. "Oh, man. I'm sorry, Greg." Injecting cheer into her voice, she continued, "I really hope it helps you get relief though!"

Greg replied warmly, "Thank you, Miss Bloom. I feel just awful that I won't help you finish."

"Don't even worry about it," she reassured him. "Besides, you've taught me so much, I'm sure I can move forward on my own."

"Yeah, that's what I'm worried about," he joked.

From anyone else, the barb might have stung, but Greg had never made her feel less than capable, despite her unconventional methods. Unlike the half-dozen other contractors she'd considered before hiring him.

"Ha ha," she said dryly. "I'll be fine. But I bet by the time you are all healed up, I'm still not done."

"They said I would be up and back to normal after six weeks, but that I probably shouldn't do ladder work or flooring for about four months."

"Four months?" Disappointment rang in her own voice. They had been making such solid progress, Daisy planned to take reservations for Valentine's Day. Good thing she hadn't told Lavender to promote it. She would already be booked—Lavender was savvy with all the marketing and promotional side of things.

"I'll see what I can do. Maybe my son—"

Daisy cut him off, "You just worry about getting better. I'll get Hawthorne to help, and we'll figure things out. Seriously," she said, "don't worry about me. Tell me where and when so I can come see you. We'll watch *This Project House*," she offered, referring to the long-running renovation show on public television. She and Greg had gotten side-tracked more than once watching clips.

"Thanks, Daisy. I really am sorry about this. I never thought it would be that bad, but the doctors were shocked I could still walk, let alone kneel."

They hung up and Daisy remained on the floor, the imperfections in the plaster ceiling blurring before her eyes with unshed tears.

It had taken her four months to find Greg. Four months of interviewing condescending and arrogant contractors who were perfectly willing to take on the project, as long as she simply sat back and looked pretty. It had been infuriating, and her pulse kicked into gear at the memory of their smug faces.

Hawthorne would help, but he had other jobs around the farm. Before she'd hired Greg, they had successfully tackled the exterior of the house. While Hawthorne was occupied elsewhere, she'd demolished the kitchen, leaving it barely functional for the two of them. That was six months ago. Unfortunately, she and Greg hadn't gotten around to the kitchen yet.

Daisy might not know how to do everything that needed done, but she could learn. That hadn't changed just because Greg wouldn't be there to teach her. Daisy opened the browser on her phone and pulled up a tutorial on installing light fixtures. She would tackle the next project herself, and since she was staring up at the ceiling, where better to start than by adding lights to the bedrooms?

Lance Matthews studied his dad across the table. Being invited to dinner at home wasn't unusual, but his dad's insistence on cooking something other than burgers definitely had him raising an eyebrow. Lance had survived childhood on chicken nuggets, Top Ramen, and whatever his dad could throw on a grill.

Unfortunately for his appetite, it was raining tonight, and Greg had attempted... what was it? Lance poked at his dinner, trying to identify the hockey puck smothered in gravy. "What's going on, Dad?"

"I'm getting my knee replaced." Greg Matthews never pulled his punches, and Lance stared at his father blankly. "In two weeks."

Puzzled, Lance replied, "Okay, good, I guess. It's been bothering you for years. It's about time you did something about it."

His dad nodded, "Yes, it is. I just wish I wasn't

leaving Miss Bloom in such a lurch." He pressed his lips together and shook his head.

"You mean the project you've been helping with out in the country? I thought it wasn't a real renovation—no crew or anything?" His dad had mentioned it a few times, but Lance didn't know the details.

"That's true. It's just me and the homeowner. But it's a special project, you know. And she's really counting on me." Head slightly bowed, Greg looked up at him and blinked.

Lance waited for the other shoe to drop. "That's too bad." He kept his voice disinterested. He wasn't falling for this. His dad hoped he would take on the project, and he refused to give in. The silence stretched, and Lance found himself biting his tongue to keep from saying the exact thing his dad waited for.

Instead, Greg sat back and started talking excitedly, "You should see the house, son. It's beautiful—original 1920s hardwoods, incredibly intricate woodwork. And I promised her I would help finish the project." His dad clicked his tongue, "I hate breaking my word."

Lance sighed, his resolve cracking. "Everyone knows you are a man of your word, Dad."

"Am I? If I was, I would figure out a way to finish

this project. Or at least hand it off to someone I trust." His dad glanced up, eyebrows raised, and Lance felt the desire to agree to the unspoken request.

Greg Matthews wouldn't beg, but he could cajole with the best of them. "Fine, Dad. You've made your point." At his dad's wide grin, Lance held up a finger. "I will go talk to the owner about it. No promises. I've got my own business to run, you know."

Greg grabbed his steak knife and tried to cut through the brick of porkchop on his plate. "That's wonderful, Lance. I knew I could count on you to make me proud. I appreciate you committing to fill my shoes." Lance started to correct his father's expansion of the promise, but it was no use. Still sawing, with little progress, his dad glanced sheepishly toward his son. "How about we go grab steaks at Lonestar?"

Lance picked up and rapped a slice of bread against the edge of his plate, giving his dad a baleful glance. "Yeah, I think that's a good call."

The following day, Lance pulled through the entrance of Bloom's Farm talking with his dad on the phone. Why was he doing this? Oh yeah, Dad practically begged him to; somehow asking without ever posing the question. Lance agreed to talk with the owner. It hardly mattered that Lance had been careful to avoid actually promising to help.

"Tell me again what you've roped me into," Lance said.

His father replied cheerfully, "You'll love it. The house is incredible. It's still got the original wood trim and everything. We already stripped the floors downstairs, and the layout is all set." Lance listened to his dad, smiling at his obvious passion for the project.

Of course, the house itself wasn't what worried him. "Okay, tell me about the owner."

"Miss Bloom likes to help. She's definitely not afraid to get her hands dirty." His dad chuckled, "It's no big deal. Just let her help and she'll let you do whatever you think is best."

Lance rolled his eyes, "So, she knows nothing and wants to watch my every move."

"Not exactly. She's smart and she wants to be involved. You'll be fine," his dad reassured him.

Unconvinced, Lance hung up the phone as he parked in front of the house. Through the windshield, he could see the historic touches. The exterior was in good shape; it even looked freshly painted.

He stepped onto the porch and rattled the obviously new stair railing. It jiggled, but not much. His dad's work?

Lance knocked, but no one answered. Stepping inside the front door, he called into the empty space, "Hello?" With wide eyes, Lance surveyed the room. The place was a disaster. One glance toward the back of the house revealed freshly framed walls with exposed wiring and nothing but subfloor. The same was true in the main living rooms, except the hardwood floor had been recently sanded. They were just asking for trouble by not having it protected during the rest of the project.

Was anything in this place finished? Piles of lumber, trim, tile and paint cans filled the open space of the living room. He wandered quietly through the hallway and found a powder room under the stairs.

Turning up the stairs, his hand trailed along the banister, and he admired the wood gleaming with fresh stain. Why on earth was this banister finished when the plaster wasn't even repaired where they'd torn down walls?

Lance called out again, "Hello? Miss Bloom?" The house remained silent, and he debated leaving. He was a professional, for crying out loud! This type of project was fine for his retired father—something to fill his days and entertain him. But Lance had real jobs to do.

Unable to resist a glimpse at the historic home, Lance looked in the first bedroom and noticed the partially removed baseboards and unfinished floors. It really was beautiful, despite the chaos. The next doorway revealed a rough-in for two bathrooms. He paced the unfinished space and realized each bathroom would attach to the adjacent bedrooms.

The layout was smart and used the space wisely. The plumbing seemed complete, with new drains running on the exterior wall. But the room was a mess, littered with scrap PVC and still-packaged vanity cabinets. Every single project appeared to be started and then abandoned. And where was Miss Bloom?

He pulled his phone out and dialed his father. "What on earth have you been doing around here?" he asked. "This place is a disaster zone. Have you lost your mind?" His dad started to object but Lance continued, "Is there even one project the two of you have finished in the last two months?"

"Miss Bloom has a bit of an unconventional approach to project scheduling," his dad said.

2

*D*aisy balanced motionless, toes poised carefully on a ceiling joist and one hand clinging to the rafter above her. When she realized there was someone in her house, she'd been curious. Her ears perked up when she heard Greg's familiar voice on the speakerphone.

The man scoffed, "Unconventional? You mean she's a loose cannon with the attention span of a gnat. The place is littered with half-finished projects. Would cleaning up a bit kill her? I could bury a small animal in the plaster dust."

Her mouth fell open in outrage, and her foot slipped off the narrow board. Circling her free arm for stability, she found her center of gravity and delicately set her toe back on the joist.

"Just because someone has a different method than you doesn't mean it won't work, son."

Exactly! At least Greg understood. Daisy liked to start new projects. What was the big deal? Everything would get done eventually. Like today's project —after watching hours of tutorials on electrical wiring, Daisy was determined to get lights added to the bedrooms. It would be much nicer to finish the flooring, walls, and trim with some actual lights. Sure, she left the baseboard job unfinished, but she was tired of pulling baseboards. That didn't mean she wasn't completely cool and capable.

"That's all well and good, but I have a real job too. Remember?"

It sounded like the man was in the bathroom, but she was several feet away in the attic above the bedroom. Even though there was no ceiling above him, his voice was muffled. Daisy leaned closer, eager to hear what the stranger was saying.

"Dad, there are people who pay me—"

With a start, she recognized the off-balance feeling in her torso and tried to catch herself. Her foot disappeared through the thick layer of loose insulation and found the wooden slats below.

With relief, she froze, wondering if her visitor heard the commotion. Did she hear him refer to

Greg as his dad? The only sound was her breathing, and the muffled sound of someone talking. He must have walked out of the bathroom. Was he in the bedroom now?

A tickle on her hand made her look up and the sight of a spider stopped her heart. Daisy shook her hand loose, immediately regretting the knee-jerk reaction as her full weight rested on the ceiling.

For a split-second, Daisy thought the plaster would hold, but it quickly gave way and she felt the cool air of the room below. Desperate not to fall eight full feet, she grabbed the next ceiling joist with her hand and stopped her descent. Loose insulation tickled the skin at her waistband, and she heard the previously muffled voice speak with new clarity.

"What the—? Um, Dad? I'll call you back later." Daisy dropped her head to her shoulder, her entire body burning with embarrassment. So much for cool and capable.

A hand gripped her calf, just above where her skinny jeans tucked into worn work boots. Stubbornly, she kicked her leg to shake off the hand. She didn't need his help.

"Whoa, whoa, whoa. Calm down there, Spirit." The man batted away her kicks and firmly grabbed her calf again when she finally calmed.

Daisy closed her eyes in resignation. There was no way to get down on her own.

The stranger called up toward her. "I'll give you a platform to push up on so you can pull your leg back up into the attic. Okay?"

With a sigh, Daisy called toward her stomach, "Okay."

"One...two...three." He applied pressure upward against her boot and she pushed against it, hauling herself safely back onto the joist.

Her own heavy breathing filled the stuffy attic. Daisy sat, unwilling to move. Maybe he would just leave. Then she wouldn't have to look at him and his smug contractor face. And it would be smug. It had been in his voice when he talked to Greg. His dad. Wasn't that what she'd heard?

How bad could he be if Greg was his father?

"Uh, lady? Are you coming down? Would you rather I come up?"

"You can leave," Daisy called down through the hole, leaning over the mess of mesh and plaster and wood to make sure her voice carried. Through the hole, she spotted a flash of skin and brown hair as he glanced up at her.

"Yeah, that's not going to happen."

Daisy tipped her head back in resignation. Of

course not. This joist wasn't exactly the most comfortable seat, the two-inch platform was digging into her butt. "Fine. I'll be down in a minute. I'll meet you in the kitchen."

LANCE STEPPED over the box of floor tile sitting in the entrance to the kitchen and sat at the tiny table tucked in the corner. With a silent laugh, he remembered the sight of the slender leg falling and dangling in mid-air, her boot-clad foot at eye-level. After his heart had restarted, he was able to process what had happened. The infamous Miss Bloom had made quite an entrance.

She nearly kicked him in the nose when she started flailing at his touch. Lance still had no idea what to expect when she came downstairs, and while his father insisted that the woman wasn't crazy, she had literally come crashing through the ceiling. If that wasn't a bad omen, he didn't know what was.

The worst part was he was still tempted to stick around. He rarely got to work on houses like this. Mostly, he spent time renovating outdated kitchens in cookie-cutter subdivisions. He would do whatever paid the bills, but this renovation was an opportunity he didn't want to pass up.

If he could tolerate a well-intentioned shadow along the way, he'd turn this old house into a beautiful testament to history. Plus, as a bed-and-breakfast, hundreds of people would see it. Maybe he could convince Miss Bloom to let him display business cards at the front desk.

Speaking of Miss Bloom, what was taking her so long? He checked his watch. Perhaps she'd gotten hurt when she fell through the ceiling. Tired of sitting, Lance wandered through the space again. On the other side of the kitchen, he found a large dining room. It was in decent shape, the flooring completed and the crown molding sanded but not stained. Same for the window trim on the gorgeous bay windows. The room would have phenomenal lighting for breakfast with guests and was big enough to seat at least ten or twelve with the right table arrangement.

Footsteps echoed behind him and he turned to catch a glimpse of the woman he would have to keep from destroying the property while he tried to renovate it. Lance wasn't sure what he expected, but the woman standing in front of him definitely was not it. Miss Bloom was younger and taller than he imagined. Despite the bits of insulation dusting her jeans and T-shirt, and the simple ponytail holding back her dark-blond hair, she was stunning.

Lance cleared his throat and asked, "Everything okay?"

Color rose in her cheeks and her eyes flashed before she responded. "All good." Then, almost reluctantly, she said, "Thanks for the lift."

He bit back a smile and nodded before sticking out his hand. "I'm Lance, by the way."

"Daisy," she said, taking a step to grasp his hand firmly. She propped a hand on her waist and tipped her head. "What are you doing here, Lance?"

"My dad said you might need help with this place, and obviously he was right," he added with a glance around the room. Lance immediately regretted the words, aware how they sounded. It was true, though. Didn't Blondie realize how far in over her head she was?

Judging by the arms now crossed over her chest and her narrowed eyes—she didn't.

"Thanks for stopping by, but I don't want your help." The ponytail swirled through the air as she whipped around and walked away.

The dismissal rankled, and he scrambled for a way to win her favor. Lance called out, "The house is gorgeous." Come on, Daisy, take the bait.

She stopped and a softer look greeted him when she turned. "Yes, it is. And I'm perfectly happy to finish it by myself. Tell your dad I hope he heals quickly."

"You'd finish it sooner if you had help," he dangled the idea, hoping she would give him a chance.

Daisy raised an eyebrow at him, "Why?"

"What?"

"Why do you want to help? I heard you on the phone. You think this place is a disaster. That I'm a disaster."

Lance tried to backpedal, "I never said that—"

"She's a loose cannon with the attention span of a gnat," she parroted in a deep parody of his voice.

Lance winced. Had he said that? "Okay, perhaps my first impression of the project was a bit... harsh." Lance stepped forward and tucked his hands in the pockets of his jeans. "I'd really love to work on this. I love historic houses, and it is really important to my dad. Together, we can bring this bed-and-breakfast to life."

Daisy pulled her lips to one side, considering his words. His gaze dropped to rest on the soft, pink skin. Quickly, he met her eyes again.

"Fine," she said, and he resisted the urge to

pump his fist like a golfer who nailed a putt, "but, I'm in charge. Got it?" She gave him a pointed look.

"Got it. Your house, your rules." Did that sound convincing? It nearly killed him to say it. Surely, he could manage Daisy Bloom and let her think she was in charge. Maybe he could divert her attention to decoration choices while he did the real work.

Daisy sighed and stared at him for another moment. Then, as if she'd come to some unspoken conclusion, she said, "I need caffeine." She shook her head and walked into the kitchen. Lance followed her and tried not to watch as she leaned into the refrigerator against an otherwise bare wall. She held up a Diet Dr. Pepper, "Want one?"

Lance declined with a shake of his head. Daisy popped the top and took a long drink, exposing her neck as she tipped her head back. He cleared his throat and asked, "So, what's your priority here?"

Daisy shrugged, her nonchalance causing irritation to flare. "Pretty much everything."

Everything can't be a priority; that was the whole point of prioritizing. He reigned in his desire to rant and asked, "What would you like to finish first?"

Daisy sipped her soda again and looked around the space. "I was running wiring in the attic to add lights to the bedroom ceilings."

Of course she was. Calamity Jane here was lucky she hadn't burned down the entire house. "Can I make a suggestion?" he asked.

She tipped her head at him to continue.

"Since you are living here while renovating, might I suggest we finish the kitchen? We could basically get the entire first floor done and then move upstairs."

"Or," she said, "we could finish the bathrooms upstairs."

How could that possibly be the best course of action? There was a working bathroom, but the kitchen was barely livable. A microwave sat on a piece of plywood and sawhorses, paper plates and pizza boxes littered the makeshift countertop. A grungy refrigerator sat against one wall, along with a utility sink haphazardly plumbed as a temporary fix.

It wasn't his house and Lance didn't have to live here though. "If you don't mind not having a kitchen, that's fine with me. But I highly recommend we start finishing some rooms."

Daisy bristled, "What is that supposed to mean?"

His pulsed jumped as he responded, "It means that by dividing your attention and trying to tackle everything at once, it takes longer and is harder than if you just finished things one room at a time." Truthfully, that was an oversimplification, but at least finish taking out the trim before deciding to hang light fixtures.

Daisy was on her feet now though, standing over him. "Look here, mister. This is my house and I will work on whatever I well please. Got it?" She pointed at him and he grabbed the offending finger.

Her hand twisted in his grasp and he released it. Lance stood, bringing himself eye to eye with her. He refused to be intimidated, but still wasn't ready to give up on working on this house. Daisy straightened as he stood, only inches between them. Once again, he was struck with her beauty, even with the fire in her eyes trying to singe him where he stood. If hitting on her wasn't akin to buying tickets on the Hot Mess Express, he would be tempted. The cute dusting of freckles on her nose confirmed she wasn't wearing makeup. Still a knock-out.

He spoke softly, "I'm just trying to offer my expertise. Why don't we walk around and you can tell me what you've got planned?"

As her temper quieted, she shrunk an inch before his eyes and he realized she'd been on her tiptoes.

"Okay," she said, "but you are on probation. And I reserve the right to fire you at any time."

"Fair enough." Daisy turned around, and Lance gave an exasperated, silent yell toward her back.

"I can see you in the window," she called, walking around the corner. Lance dropped his hands and found his own reflection in the kitchen window. Maybe this wasn't such a great idea. They'd known each other for twenty minutes and he was already losing it.

3

*D*aisy walked her new contractor through the house, pointing out what she'd completed and sharing the seemingly endless list of what still needed to be done. In each room, she reminded herself to ignore the handsome cut of his jawline and the way his T-shirt pulled across his chest when he gestured to the ceiling or windows. Lance Matthews might be handsome, but he was everything she didn't want in a man. That was obvious in the way he studied the chaos with disdain. Daisy would never be a neat freak, and her creativity flourished within flexible boundaries. Or no boundaries at all.

Even so, it pained her to admit that Lance might be right. There wasn't a single room in the house completely finished. Maybe that was one reason she'd been getting discouraged with the project.

She loved starting new things. Daisy had jumped from one hobby to the next her entire life, never sticking with anything—except dancing. Dancing had been everything to her until an untimely injury ended her time with the professional dance troupe.

By the end of the tour, Daisy was holding back a wince with every careful footstep. The leg that had crashed through the ceiling must have taken a harder impact than she thought.

Back in the entryway, she held open her hands, "That's it. You've seen the whole house."

Lance looked around at the grand entryway, "It really is a beautiful house, Daisy. Thanks for letting me work on it with you." Pride swelled within her at his words. This dream of hers was really happening, and it still amazed her.

For a month after finishing the front porch, she spent every spare moment on the Adirondack chairs enjoying the fruits of her labor, and had been energized to continue working the long days required. Maybe she needed a victory like that inside the house to bring back the joy. Elation from starting something new only lasted a moment, but triumph of finishing lingered.

Daisy shrugged, "Don't thank me yet. I know I'm a pain, because half a dozen other contractors refused to let me be as involved as I want to be. I expect you to talk me through your decisions and teach me how to do what you are doing."

He nodded, "I'm good with that."

It seemed they'd reached an understanding along the way. Maybe this wouldn't be so bad. Lance seemed to know what he was talking about, even if he had picked up discarded boxes in each room and tossed them in a trash bag. Daisy could deal with a clean workspace—as long as she wasn't the one cleaning it up.

"Great." She shifted her weight to ease her aching ankle and said, "Let's start fresh next week. How often will you come? Your dad was coming about three days a week."

After considering, Lance replied, "I'll check on my other projects to be sure. I'll let you know." They exchanged phone numbers and finally, he left. She'd been unwilling to show the weakness when he was there, but now that he was gone, Daisy pulled off her boot with a wince. Bruises were already forming on her calf where it had scraped on the wood slats.

More attic adventures would have to wait. For now, Daisy needed to talk to someone about what just happened. It was times like these she missed Andi the most. With her twin sister halfway around the world in the Army, emails and video calls were a poor substitute for a real-life chat. Poppy would be around somewhere though; she almost never left the farm.

Daisy drove to the pole barn that acted as Poppy's base of operations for the organic produce portion of Bloom's Farm. For as long as Daisy could remember, her father set up stands at local farmers' markets selling apples, sweetcorn, and watermelons, eventually broadening to include other produce. All the Blooms spent early mornings picking produce and loading up the pickup during the growing season. Poppy had a few farmhands who helped, but even now, anyone with free hands pitched in during the busy season. Produce was still the cornerstone of Bloom's Farm, with the fall apple-picking events at the orchards adding a new family-friendly event for the local area.

When Daisy poked her head in, Poppy wasn't in her makeshift office. Her farmhand, Clint, said he hadn't seen her. With a sigh, Daisy drove to the main house instead; maybe Poppy was there. If nothing else, Daisy would find her mother in the office or Lavender on her computer. That was one nice thing about having such a big family. With six siblings, Daisy always had someone to talk to.

The railing supported her weight as she hobbled up the front steps of the main house. Her parents built this house just before Daisy and Andi were born. Good thing, too, because the old house only had one bathroom. It had been hard enough competing for the mirror with three bathrooms and six girls.

The main house had been home, except for her time in New York and since moving into the old house to renovate it. Sometimes Daisy wondered if moving back to the farm after her broken ankle had been the easy way out, but after her dream of dancing died, she was aimless. Plus, there was always work to do around here. As the oldest, Lily had been ready for her own space right away, and of course Andi was a million miles away. But everyone else was still around the farm. Lily kept her apartment in Terre Haute, even after her job as an event coordinator at a local restaurant was replaced with running Storybook Barn full-time.

The living room and kitchen were empty, which meant her mom was holed up in the room they used as an office. Daisy sneaked past the closed door, not wanting to get roped into a conversation about invoices and income statements. Budgets and balance sheets were to be avoided at all costs.

Daisy stopped in the doorway of Lavender's room, spying on her younger sister as she chattered to a camera stationed above her computer. Bright lights illuminated Lavender's face as she held up a package to the camera and Daisy rolled her eyes. Another video?

Not knowing if her sister was recording or broadcasting live, Daisy waited outside until Lavender finished. Daisy almost gave up, but the screen on the computer stopped showing Lavender's face and she turned around, jolting in her seat when she noticed Daisy leaning against the door frame.

"Oh!" An embarrassed blush covered her face and Lavender asked, "How long have you been there?"

Daisy raised an eyebrow and teased, "Long enough to see you playing fashion icon." Annoyance flickered across her sister's face and Daisy's conscience twinged. They all had their hobbies, right?

Lavender stood and took off the belted jacket she was wearing, revealing a cute tunic underneath. Unsurprisingly, the outfit was adorable, and Daisy said as much to her sister.

"Thanks, I got it on sale." Lavender studied Daisy's face. "Why aren't you at the old house?"

Daisy flopped on her sister's green bedspread and unloaded her current troubles. The words spilled out, about how Greg couldn't help and had, oh by the way, forced his incredibly frustrating son to take his place.

While she talked, Lavender swapped pants and added a fancy belt to the tunic, then layered a different cardigan over the outfit, each time snapping pictures with the camera set on a tripod. Once Daisy had exhausted her list of frustrations, she gave her sister a skeptical look. "What are you doing?"

Lavender flipped through her closet and said absently, "I'm doing a blog post and video about capsule wardrobes." She turned to Daisy, "If you don't want his help, why don't you just tell Lance to take a hike?"

Daisy groaned and pulled a pillow over her head. "I fell through the ceiling," she admitted.

Muffled snickers came from the closet and then Lavender let out a full laugh, "Come again?"

Daisy threw the pillow at her sister. "Forget it," she said and stood up.

"No, no, don't go," Lavender laughed.

Composing herself, her face grew serious, "Are you okay?"

"My leg is a little bruised, but mostly my ego, I think." That was the crux of it, since Daisy didn't think she'd ever been more embarrassed in her life. "I don't really like the guy, and I already humiliated myself in front of him. But I'm afraid I won't be able to make this happen without his help."

Lavender gave her a hug. Then, stepping out of arm's reach, she asked, "Is he at least cute?"

Daisy's mouth fell open with a surprised laugh at her sister's comment and she reached behind her for another pillow to throw.

Lavender held up her arms to block the projectile, "What? I'm just saying, if you've got to work with this guy, the least he could do is provide a little extra scenery!" Then she looked at Daisy's expression and her eyes widened. "Oh my goodness, he really is cute, isn't he?" she said victoriously.

At their fit of laughter, Laura Bloom stuck her head around the corner with a smile. "What is going on in here, girls?"

"Daisy's new contractor is eye candy!" Lavender shouted with glee, and Daisy buried her burning face in her hands.

"No, no! That's not true." She looked up and

continued with a stern voice, "What he is, actually, is rigid and annoying and smug." There, that was better. Just because he was handsome and knew his way around a construction site didn't erase the negatives. And Daisy would not let herself forget it.

4

*L*ance left Bloom's farm with a smile on his face. Whatever one could say about Daisy Bloom, she wasn't boring. Still, he was skeptical about working alongside someone so disorganized and potentially unsafe. Seriously, who fell through the ceiling?

Lance needed to make sure his insurance was paid up while working this job, just in case Daisy dropped a two-by-four on his head. She definitely tested his patience. He said a quick prayer about that particular struggle. He hadn't exactly put his best foot forward when talking to his new employer.

Even if he was doing this project for the selfish reasons of wanting to work on the historic property, she was technically the boss. Lance grimaced, remembering her plan of attack to finish the upstairs first. It wouldn't be terrible, except her ability to focus on one thing at a time was nearly nonexistent. If he could at least channel her energy into smaller areas, the place wouldn't take long to finish.

He called his dad as he covered the last few miles on his way into Greencastle.

"You left already? Don't tell me she kicked you out."

"She had a bit of a rough morning. I'll head back out tomorrow, but I'll take the job. So, you can get off my back."

"Oh good. She's a good girl, and she told me about all the contractors who didn't treat her with the respect a woman deserves. Downright shameful, some of them. I sure hoped you wouldn't be that kind of man."

His fingers clinched the steering wheel at the thought of Daisy interviewing contractors, many who he knew personally and would never introduce to his sister. If he had a sister, that is. "You know I'd never do anything disrespectful," he said, then considered what Daisy had overheard on the phone. "Well, not like you mean, anyway."

Thankfully, his dad didn't catch his comment and asked, "What did you think of the house?"

Lance gave his impression of the property and admitted to his dad he was excited to work on it.

"Hah, I knew you would be. You and I are the same, boy. I might be older and mellower, but we've still got a few things in common." Lance smiled at his dad's exuberance.

"We sure do, Dad. Look, I've got to run into this other project and check on my guys. I'll check in with you tomorrow."

They said goodbye, and he grabbed his hardhat from the floorboard of the passenger seat, tucking his phone into the pocket of his jeans after he stepped down from the truck cab. This house was a complete overhaul. An investor had bought the property at auction and the entire thing needed a facelift—new carpet, paint, fixtures, bathrooms, and kitchen. The guy would turn around and sell it for a profit. At least, that was always the plan.

Lance preferred his own lower-risk business plan. No matter what happened with housing prices, he would be paid for the work he did. While he knew the investors could make a quick buck, he'd also seen them lose their shirt, and Lance was too careful for that.

With a wave at a subcontractor in the driveway, Lance walked up to the front door and into the house. Already, the house was dramatically different, with the ratty carpet removed and a wall opened up in the kitchen. He found Cody, his foreman for the project, hanging new, sleek white cabinets where the originals had been removed. With the new layout, the space had a clean, modern look.

Lance despised the stark lines and overwhelming white, but his investor had a vision—or his investor's girlfriend did. Lance grabbed a screw and handed it to Cody so he could drive it into the back panel to secure the cabinet to the wall. "How's it going around here?"

After the short whir from the drill, Cody pulled his body out of the cabinet shell and stepped off the step ladder. "It's good. Plumber said he's about finished. Then we can get the tile work done and finish the bathrooms." Lance looked around and noticed the clean workspace with satisfaction. The crew had finished drywalling and unpackaged cabinetry, yet no trace of the drywall dust or packing materials lingered in the space—drastically different from Crazy Daisy's house of horrors.

"Sounds good. When does the tile guy come?"

Cody winced. "Actually, Adrian bailed again. I'll have to do it or find somebody else."

Lance sighed. Adrian was their best tile expert,

but he was becoming more and more unreliable. "I'll see if anybody has recommendations. If all else fails, you and I can tackle it together. Maybe spend some time training Jamie on the basics," he said, referring to the newest member of their crew. Jamie was eager to learn and picked up new skills quickly. Plus, he was detail-oriented, which was exactly what Lance wanted with someone laying tile.

Cody turned to him, "What's the word at the new job?"

Lance rolled his eyes. "I don't know what my dad was thinking. Actually," he interjected, "I do, because it's the same thing I am. The house is amazing. 1920s, original woodwork, stained glass accent windows. It's really incredible."

"But...?" They'd been working together for too long, clearly.

"But the homeowner wants to be involved."

Cody's look turned to one of confusion. "Don't most of them? That's why I'm hanging these hideous cabinets, isn't it?"

Lance laughed and replied, "They are pretty bad, aren't they? But no, Miss Bloom doesn't want to just select materials. Renovation Barbie wants to help."

Cody's laughter echoed in the nearly empty

space, "What's the big deal? Let her swing a hammer until she gets bored and then finish it yourself."

Lance pulled off his hardhat and rubbed his forehead with his arm. "Yeah, that was my plan. But this morning she was in the attic pulling new cable."

Impressed, Cody's eyes widened and he tipped his head from side to side as if weighing the options. "Good for her."

Lance grunted, but didn't tell Cody the rest of the story, not wanting to embarrass Daisy. Why did he even care what Cody thought about her? Somehow, he knew it would kill Daisy to think she was a joke to him. After walking through the house with her and seeing what she had tackled on her own, he was impressed.

She might be unconventional, but Daisy wasn't afraid to tackle things or work hard. She was in the attic, after all, which meant she was serious about doing this.

"Anyway, she wants to help, but she doesn't know a ton. It'll be a time-sink for me over the next few months. I'm not convinced it's a great decision business-wise. But," with a bend of his knees, he gave Cody a dramatic look of ecstasy, "the house, man. I have to do it."

Cody laughed. "It's all good, dude. I can pretty

much hold down the fort here and I'm sure Jason has the smaller projects managed."

Lance nodded. He had a good team, built one careful hire at a time over the last eight years. They always made sure his company honored its reputation for quality work. "I'll be here a couple of mornings a week until we get wrapped up and move on to Riverside Boulevard. I told them we'd start after Thanksgiving."

"Roger. Give me a hand with this next cabinet?"

Lance and Cody hung the upper cabinets while the plumber finished up and the other crew members painted the bedrooms and rolled out new carpets. All the while, though, Lance's thoughts were centered about twenty minutes straight west, at the home of a surprisingly beautiful and equally frustrating woman.

5

On Saturday morning, Daisy and Hawthorne drove up to the main house together. Brunch was the one mandatory family event every week. Even Andi barely got out of the commitment, and she was stationed overseas.

Inside the house, the familiar smell of cinnamon rolls and bacon greeted Daisy, and sure enough, when they turned the corner, her mom was icing a full tray of the giant pastries.

While Hawthorne teased their mother and inquired about coffee, Daisy walked directly to the fridge and pulled open the bottom vegetable drawer, pushing aside a bag of carrots to uncover her stash of Diet Dr. Pepper.

"Ah-hah!"

With a look of horror, Hawthorne asked, "Isn't it too early for that?"

As if everyone here wasn't well aware of her addiction. It just so happened that she was out at the old house, otherwise she would have already had one today. With a cheerful, "Never!" she tucked one foot up onto the bar stool and rested the open can on her leg.

Daisy sat and sipped her drink as the motion of the morning picked up around her. Poppy wandered in, looking for their dad, and Lavender came in from the garage holding orange juice.

As Lavender set the table, their mom spoke up, "We've got an extra this morning, Lovey. Could you set the table for eight?"

Eyebrows rose around the kitchen, but Hawthorne was the first to speak. "Who's coming? Is Andi back in town?" Daisy's heart skipped with anticipation. A surprise visit from her twin sister would be a dream come true. It wasn't fair that Andi had to be so far away.

"I wish," her mother said. "No, actually I ran into an old friend at the grocery store and invited her to join us. Do you all remember Avery Chase?"

Daisy straightened, "Oh my goodness, Avery is back?" Avery had been one of her best friends in junior high and high school, until she'd moved away in 11th grade. "Poppy, do you remember that time Avery and you tipped the golf cart?" Poppy laughed at the memory and they started exchanging stories. Daisy couldn't believe Avery was back. It had been, what, thirteen years?

Lavender added a memory, "What about the time you guys got Hawthorne and Josh with water balloons from the hayloft?" Daisy laughed out loud at the memory of the prank. As Lavender finished talking, Rose walked in from the laundry room and pulled off her boots. "Good morning, everybody."

Greetings for their youngest sister filled the kitchen and she made her way toward the living room complaining about one of the dogs smearing her with something gross.

"I don't smell anything other than your usual delightful scent, sis," Hawthorne teased and Rose responded with a swat to the back of his head. When he winced, Daisy absently wondered if he had a hangover this morning. She hadn't noticed him coming in late this week. Come to think of it, Hawthorne had been home every night this week. What was up with that?

Lavender gave an exaggerated gag. "Gross. I'm so glad I don't have to help with animals anymore."

Daisy sat up straight and gave a silent exaggeration reenactment of her sister's girly-girl attitude behind her back, twirling her hair and showing mock disgust at imaginary dirt on her hands. Across the room, Poppy hid a laugh behind her coffee cup.

A knock on the front door sounded—Avery! Daisy jumped up and exclaimed, "I'll get it!" before jogging to the door. She threw it open and the mature, yet familiar face of her old friend greeted her.

"Ah! I can't believe you are back," she said, running in place with excitement. With another short exclamation, Daisy pulled Avery inside and into a big hug. "Come on in, you have to come see everyone!"

Over brunch, Avery shared what she had been doing for last thirteen years. She was a chemical engineer and doing research at the university with Dr. Pike, Mandy's father. In light of Avery's success, Daisy couldn't help but feel a bit unaccomplished, but the pride in her ongoing project still made her want to share. Plus, there had been some seriously interesting vibes between Hawthorne and Avery that Daisy needed to dig into more.

After brunch with the family, Daisy invited Avery back to the B&B for a tour. They left the main house and jumped into Avery's car for the short drive back to the homestead. After she parked in front, Avery exclaimed, "Wow, Daze! This looks incredible." Daisy's heart warmed at the praise and the old nickname.

"Thank you! There was just something about getting the exterior done that made it feel more attainable. The inside is essentially a war zone," Daisy joked.

When they walked in, Avery studied the space and gestured to the left, "Didn't there used to be a wall here?"

Daisy laughed. "Good memory! This used to be the front parlor. And then this was the living room. But I wanted it to be one big space instead. Greg, my contractor, was able to install a beam and take out the wall."

"Wow, that's awesome. Floors?"

Daisy bent down and rubbed her hand on the narrow wood boards. "Mostly original, with a few patches. As long as I can convince Lance to teach me how to patch them."

Avery raised an eyebrow. "Lance?"

Daisy stood and let out a growl, "Lance is Greg's son. And apparently Greg has to get his knee replaced. Which means he asked his far-more-infuriating son and business partner to manage the project. He was here for the first time the other day." Daisy took a deep breath and reminded herself to be gracious. Lance hadn't actually done anything. Yet. But just because the plane hadn't crashed yet didn't mean you couldn't see the mountain coming.

Daisy exhaled and turned to the kitchen. "Anyway, I don't want to talk about Lance," she said, spitting out his name. She forced a smile and said, "Come look at the kitchen. It's coming along."

Daisy showed her friend the kitchen and then they went upstairs. Avery's reaction to the retro bathroom she and Hawthorne were currently sharing was hilarious. The baby-blue tile and matching blue bathtub were definitely eye-catching.

After the tour, they sat at the small table tucked in the corner of the kitchen, the same place she'd sat with Lance a few days prior. Avery took her up on the offer of a Diet Dr. Pepper.

"It's so good to have you back, Avery."

Avery smiled and grabbed her hand. "It's really good to be back. I'm sorry I didn't stay in touch."

"Don't be," Daisy waved her soda. "We were kids and it was probably unrealistic to think we would."

"Well, that doesn't change the fact that I wish we had."

"Doesn't matter now. We can make up for lost time." Daisy thought about her plans for the week before saying, "Poppy and I have a movie night planned on Thursday. Want to come?"

Avery agreed to come and Daisy started planning the evening. After being covered in construction dust all day, and especially since Lance would be here all week, she would definitely need some good old-fashioned girl time.

Hawthorne walked into the kitchen, and Daisy raised her eyebrow at his wild, wide-eyed look.

Avery sat up straight and stammered, "I-I should go."

"Whoa, whoa. You don't have to—" she started to say, but Avery was already dumping her soda into the sink and gathering her scarf and coat.

Across the room, Hawthorne spoke up. "Sure, just run out again without giving me a chance."

Again? Completely entranced by the drama, Daisy froze.

"Do you have something you'd like to say, Hawthorne?" Avery raised her chin and spoke clearly, almost daring him to continue.

Hawthorne ran a hand through his dark, wind-blown hair. Finally, he answered, "Can I walk you out?"

Daisy's eyes widened and she covered her mouth, suddenly open with a gasp at the fireworks before her. What was happening right now? Avery turned back to Daisy and wrapped her in a quick hug. "I'll see you and Poppy later this week, okay?"

"Sounds good," she replied absently, still watching them both with intense interest before walking behind Avery. "Be nice," she mouthed to Hawthorne.

Daisy paused on the steps and heard Hawthorne let out a sigh before saying, "Shall we?"

There was definitely something going on. Between the absolute avoidance of Hawthorne at brunch and his cryptic comment about not getting a chance, Daisy was missing all kinds of information. Thursday couldn't come soon enough.

6

*M*onday morning, Lance found Daisy in the upstairs bedroom. At least she'd abandoned her plans for wiring new lights by herself. She'd finished removing the baseboards and was sanding the corners of the newly stripped floors. Apparently, Barb Vila had a productive weekend.

"Floors are in good shape," he said by way of greeting, biting back a smile when she jumped at his voice.

Sheepishly, she removed an earbud and let it hang from her shoulder. "Sorry, I didn't hear you."

"No worries. Looks like you had a busy weekend," he gestured to the now naked wood.

Daisy nodded, "Yeah, I had some free time. And

your dad was good about teaching me how to use the sander when we did the first floor."

They made a plan for the day, and even though Lance didn't like leaving the kitchen untouched, they would focus their efforts on getting two bedrooms and attached bathrooms completed. The list became too much to remember, and Lance pulled out the small notebook he always kept in the front pocket of his plaid shirt.

With a raise eyebrow, Daisy smirked. "No pocket protector?"

"Only on Sundays," he quipped, pleased when he made her laugh. The transformation was amazing when the guarded, ready-for-battle expression on her face was replaced with one of joy.

They ran through the list again as Lance took notes. He copied it again, this time in order of what they should do, while Daisy fidgeted impatiently across the room. More than once she tried interrupting, but he deflected. At one point, she got up and returned a minute later with a can of soda.

After the list was complete, Lance tried to figure out how to give his opinion without offending her. Finally, he settled on compliments first, suggestions second.

"Everything you've done so far looks fantastic."

Daisy rolled her eyes at the praise and Lance cleared his throat nervously but continued, "I might not agree with the methods or the order you've tackled things—but I can't argue with the quality of your work." Truth be told, her work was better than some guys on his crew. The trim was carefully removed, preserving each piece so it could be reinstalled after the flooring was finished. Even the hardwoods, which were easy to damage with the large sander, looked like they were done by a professional.

Still, getting her on board with his plan would make the entire project run more smoothly. "You are in charge, and unless it is impossible, I'll work with what you want to do. But here is what I would recommend." He laid out an order of operations—starting with electrical in the baths and bedrooms, followed by drywall, showers and flooring in the bathrooms. Then it was a matter of finishing touches and trim for the two rooms to be complete.

While he laid out his plan, Daisy nodded along and came closer to look at the list with him. She asked questions—good ones, if he was being honest. The most disconcerting thing was the way his body reacted to her proximity.

Despite her simple T-shirt and messy ponytail, Daisy was gorgeous. When she looked at him with actual respect and kindness? He was in all sorts of trouble. Clearing his throat, Lance stood and brushed the fine sawdust from his jeans.

"Do you have everything for the electrical?"

"Just the wiring. I haven't picked up junction boxes or switches."

"Okay," he said, "you want to run to the hardware store while I run the wire? We'll install the boxes together when you get back."

They discussed outlets and switches for the rooms and then, Diet Dr. Pepper in hand, Daisy headed out. The house was strangely silent after she left; as though even when she wasn't making noise, Daisy filled the space with life.

Lance shook his head and dismissed the poetic notion. He was being ridiculous. This was just a job, and he needed to get to work.

DAISY HATED TO ADMIT IT, but she already felt better having someone who knew what they were doing. She'd learned so much between Hawthorne and Greg and the videos she found online. There was still something daunting about staring at the blank slate of bare framing and tackling it by herself.

She held no disappointment that Lance would go into the attic and run the wires, either. Daisy wanted to help with the installation of the lights and bathroom fans though. After a dozen videos on that particular task, she was eager to try for herself.

Daisy thanked the cashier, one she was becoming familiar with as the project progressed, and drove back to the farm. The bags of light switches, outlets and junction boxes bumped her legs as she went up the stairs. Stepping through the gap between two framing studs, Daisy's eyes widened at the sight in front of her. Strong legs, wrapped in sturdy denim jeans, met a plaid shirt just above the pockets. Pockets that accentuated the firm shape of Lance's rear end, positioned directly at eye level. His shoulders disappeared above the ceiling, and he was tugging wire through a hole in the joist.

Wanting to enjoy the view a moment longer, she set down the bags quietly and stood back. Seeing Lance on a ladder shouldn't be this enjoyable, should it? Still, without the attitude and the obnoxious neat freak brain attached, maybe Lance wasn't so bad.

Daisy felt her face grow hot when he moved. The boots slowly descended, and the rest of his torso, shoulders and head came into view. Guess it was time to get back to work.

Lance turned around and spotted her, "Oh good, you're back. Just in time. I just finished feeding the wire in the attic. We should be good to hook everything up." His face grew puzzled, and Daisy realized she was still staring. Thankfully, her gaze was unfocused, no longer looking at anything specific, but she pulled herself into the moment.

"What?" she asked, hearing but not understanding the words he'd spoken.

Lance looked at her skeptically, "Not enough caffeine this morning?"

What was she doing? This was her contractor, and Daisy couldn't stand the guy or his overly organized tendencies. Unfortunately, he was also strong and capable and, most of the time, polite—the exact qualities she so often lamented lacking in the men she met. Daisy absolutely could not develop a crush on Lance Matthews. She just needed to focus on the project and definitely resist the urge to stare at his forearms as they pulled open the plastic packaging on the electrical supplies. It didn't matter that with his sleeves rolled up to his elbows, she could see the lean muscles ripple under his tanned skin.

He must spend a lot of time outside. Did he have a farmer's tan like her father and brother, with upper arms dramatically more pale? She always made fun of Hawthorne when she spotted his bare biceps in stark contrast to his forearms. Sometimes he worked without a shirt on to even it out. Did Lance ever work without a shirt?

Daisy's face flushed. It doesn't matter if he does, and he better not do it at this house. That was the last thing she needed to worry about.

Lance Matthews might be handsome and respectful, but he was rigid and controlling, and Daisy would not give her heart to someone who expected it to be neatly wrapped. She was messy. Not just her room—although Hawthorne had threatened to throw everything away if he walked by, unable to see the floor again. Daisy herself was messy. Her dreams had taken a rambling path to New York and back, and her emotions flared in wild ups and downs, passionate reactions to whatever was happening. Lance had probably set his life goals when he was seven and never veered more than a step from the path he'd laid out. The only thing that got Lance riled up was something that didn't fit his perfect plan.

And Daisy did not fit there.

If only she didn't enjoy riling him up so much.

WHEN LANCE ARRIVED at the house the next afternoon, soaring music greeted him loudly. Wincing at
the volume, he walked upstairs and into the north
bedroom. The scene he saw there was equally unsur-
prising and entertaining.

Daisy stood near the wall, paint roller in hand.
Instead of using it to deposit the pale green color
onto the walls, she was singing the classic love ballad
at the top of her lungs—still barely audible over the
stereo—and using the handle of her roller as a micro-
phone. The words spoke of love lost and dreams
unrealized. Heartbreak laced with hope. Lance
debated whether he should interrupt her. Then the
chorus ended, and the instrumental break began.

Lance watched, struck into total stillness as
Daisy transformed before his eyes. She bent—no, she
folded—in half, melting at the waist, and set the
roller in the tray. Her arms extended over her head,
and Daisy began to dance.

Her eyes were closed, her slender neck and arms
raised. Daisy was absolutely absorbed in the music
and the music seemed to flow from within her.

It only took a few moments, maybe thirty
seconds, but Lance couldn't move. Couldn't breathe.

Daisy spun gracefully, her body twisting and
billowing as if blown by the breeze, or on strings held

by a master puppeteer. It wasn't typical dance music, not in his mind. But the ballad had strings soaring in graceful crescendos that took the listener on a journey, notes crashing and subsiding until giving way to the next part of the song.

The chorus started again and Daisy opened her eyes, quickly wiping them with the back of her hand. They widened in shock and Lance watched, still frozen, as her expression changed from bliss to shock, and finally to anger.

"Get out."

"Daisy, that was—"

"I said get out!" she yelled, walking towards him and trying to push him out of the room.

Lance tried to find the words. He knew he'd just seen Daisy. He'd seen the innermost vulnerable piece of the woman he'd been working alongside. "Beautiful," he finished.

Daisy's forceful shoves stopped, and she looked up at him. Lance met her eyes, seeing the moisture still gathered there and the tracks of the tears she'd wiped away. She made herself cry by dancing? It had been profoundly moving just to watch. How much more so must it be to channel that emotion into your body and release it through dance? Another layer to Daisy was unraveling before him, like the loose string on a knit sweater, and Lance wanted nothing more than to pull on the thread and watch it reveal what was underneath. What was her story?

Somehow, he'd assumed she was just another spoiled daughter of a successful farmer. Daisy was living on her parents' property and didn't seem to have any responsibilities beyond the house they were standing in. "I'm sorry I didn't make my presence known sooner. But I'm not sorry I saw you dancing. It was... incredible."

Instinctively, he brushed a piece of hair and dried the moisture at her temple with his thumb. Her eyes drifted closed and Lance's breath caught in his throat. What was he doing? Kissing Daisy was the last thing he should be doing. But it was all he could think about. His gaze stumbled on her lips and he licked his own as his mouth went dry as a creek in July.

Instead of doing exactly what his heart was telling him to, Lance stepped back and tried not to notice if Daisy wore a look of disappointment when she opened her eyes.

Desperate to change the subject, Lance looked around the room. It had come a long way since his first visit. For one, the hole where Daisy had fallen through the ceiling was patched. There was a new ceiling fan and light fixture, and they had installed the door to the ensuite bathroom. After the painting was complete, they just needed to stain the floor and reinstall the baseboards.

"I like the color," he said. It was a lame excuse for a conversation starter, but he knew he would never see that shade of green again without picturing Daisy in her yoga pants, the curve and sway of her body hypnotic and full of emotion. He didn't realize a dance could convey so much heartache. But Daisy had ripped open her soul and artfully spilled it out on the unfinished hardwood floor.

Lance was not creative. Almost proudly, he proclaimed his inability to carry a tune in a bucket or to tell a Monet from a Manet. He'd never been to a ballet, and musicals or plays all seemed hokey to him.

But Tiny Dancer over there?

Yeah, he could gladly watch that again.

7

_D_aisy opened the door when Avery knocked and thrust her trusty caboodle makeup case at her. She hollered at her mom and dad before leading her friend downstairs with an armful of snacks and a bottle of wine. Daisy was dying to ask Avery what happened with Hawthorne on Saturday, but she needed to wait until the time was right.

When they went downstairs, Poppy and Mandy Elliot were waiting. Mandy glanced at the hot pink and teal tote, still wearing the stickers and fingernail polish art from their preteen years and raised her eyebrow. Mandy had been friends with the girls since childhood, and now ran her own daycare in Minden.

"Honestly, Daisy. Aren't we too old for a caboodle?"

"Speak for yourself. I saw some for sale the other day at Walmart, believe it or not. The nineties are back, baby!" Daisy pumped a fist in the air in celebration.

Poppy flipped through movies on the streaming app and Daisy asked, "Find anything good?"

Her sister kept scrolling. "We could watch the new Ryan Gosling movie, or this one about bridesmaids?"

Daisy frowned. Ryan Gosling looked a little too similar to a particular contractor she was hoping to forget for a few hours. "How about we embrace the nineties theme tonight and watch something older?"

They settled on a classic romantic comedy and got comfortable.

Munching on chips, Daisy glanced at Avery then back to the movie, debating if Avery would spill her guts yet. Maybe more wine would help. Avery turned, grabbed a chip, and asked pointedly, "Do you have a question?"

"Who, me?" Daisy tried to play innocent, but Avery didn't fall for it.

"Yes, you. You are practically vibrating over

there." Poppy was engrossed in the movie but finally turned around when Daisy paused the movie.

At Poppy's outburst, Daisy held up the remote. "I'll turn it back on in a second. There are more pressing matters. Like whatever Avery and Hawthorne needed to discuss privately after brunch." Daisy poured them each a glass of wine, ready to hear the scoop.

"Ooooh! I want to know, too," Mandy turned away from the TV to face them.

Avery's insisted it was nothing, but Daisy needled further. Asking her friend about the sparks flying on Saturday was the most important thing on her agenda tonight.

Daisy laughed, "Come on. We all know you had a huge crush on him back in the day." Avery had a desperate crush on Hawthorne, even if she hid it well.

Avery's mouth dropped open, "You knew?"

Poppy interjected this time. "Of course we knew! Half our friends had a crush on Hawthorne."

"It's true. I totally did," Mandy admitted with a laugh. "And if any of you tell Garrett that, I'll vehemently deny it. I bet I can get Lily to back me up." Daisy's heart warmed at Mandy's infatuation with her fiancé. Not even a year ago, Mandy was convinced she would be alone forever. God had other plans, and Dr. Garrett Pike had entered her story.

When Avery shared how she'd run into Hawthorne and his group of dumb friends in Terre Haute, the light of understanding finally came on. Daisy knew the basics of how Hawthorne spent his time; she wasn't totally naïve. The doofus slept in the room next to hers, when he bothered to come home at all.

Avery admitted to scolding Hawthorne and his friends for their obnoxious behavior, and Daisy couldn't hold in the laugh that rose up at the mental picture. "That's amazing. I wish I could have seen the look on his face."

When Avery explained that Hawthorne hadn't recognized her and she hadn't shared who she was, they cracked up. Now, his reaction at brunch and the tense undertones made so much sense. Good for Avery though. Someone needed to knock some sense into Hawthorne. Daisy had tried, but his defensive attitude made it hard to get through. Instead, she'd been praying for him every day. Lately, Hawthorne had been around a lot more, with no more late nights.

She asked Avery, "When did you say this

happened?"

"Friday before last." Almost two weeks. Daisy thought through the last few weeks—the timeline matched.

With a shrug, she told Avery, "For what it's worth, I don't think he's gone out with those friends again since then." Maybe Avery's brief confrontation was the push he needed. Avery brushed off her comment and they restarted the movie.

A second later, Daisy leaned over and whispered, "He's a good man, Avery." Daisy loved Hawthorne. When it counted, her brother always came through. His friends were less than desirable, but maybe meeting Avery made a difference. He'd certainly been easier to live with.

After the movie, they chose colors for their nails and started talking again. Daisy asked about Avery's little sister, Brie, and while each painted their own toenails, Mandy asked Daisy about the renovation.

"Actually, we are making really good progress. Lance might be infuriating and uptight, but he knows his stuff."

Poppy perked up. "Infuriating and uptight, huh? What does he do to irritate you?"

Daisy rolled her eyes, "What doesn't he do to irritate me? The man is constantly cleaning up behind me and making lists. He insists we finish one thing before starting something else." Feeling eyes on her, Daisy looked up from her purple-painted toes to see blank looks from her sister and friends. "What?"

"Yes, that sounds dreadful," Poppy remarked sarcastically.

Avery nodded, "How do you live with someone who cleans?" She said the word with horror and Poppy and Mandy burst into laughter.

"Ha-ha," Daisy said dryly. "Very funny. I'm serious, guys. He makes me crazy."

"So fire him," Mandy suggested.

The idea had occurred to Daisy. But not seeing Lance was actually kind of depressing. Maybe he had driven her insane. She liked having him around? At the realization, heat rose in her cheeks.

"Oh my gosh," Poppy's head snapped up, "You like him!"

Daisy shook her head in denial, "I don't. He's the worst."

Mandy and Poppy looked at each other and chorused, "Me thinks the lady doth protest too much!" causing Daisy to laugh and her cheeks to grow hotter.

"Ack, you guys are the worst, too."

Once they recovered from their giggles, Poppy

asked, "Seriously, Daze. When was the last time you had a date?"

Daisy straightened, taken aback by the question. "It's been a while, but—"

"I'm pretty sure it's been like five years." Why was she cursed with sisters who couldn't mind their own business?

"So what? We both know the dating game around here is pathetic. And I don't need to date to be happy!" Daisy always figured God would make it happen when it was time. Mandy had tried online dating and her other friends spent nights frequenting the singles' groups at church..

Daisy had family and friends and now, her bed-and-breakfast. She did not need to date to be complete. Take her oldest sister, Lily—Lily never dated and was perfectly happy. Maybe a bit intense, but that didn't mean she was pining away for a man to rescue her. And neither was Daisy.

Poppy nodded, "I never said you did. I'm just saying maybe you are mistaking chemistry for incompatibility."

Daisy shook her head. "Nope. Lance Matthews is the exact opposite of the kind of man I would ever fall for." She gave a dramatic shudder of disgust. "Can you imagine? He doesn't have a creative bone in his body." Poppy was definitely mistaken. They didn't have chemistry. What they had was a completely opposite approach to life. He was boring and neat; she was fun and creative. That was a recipe for disaster.

She'd already given up her dancing, and it had almost crushed her. Getting involved with Lance would be a nightmare of lists and schedules, and there was no way Daisy would do that. No way at all.

8

Finally, the electrical work was done and the drywall complete. Daisy rubbed her hands together eagerly; today was a day she'd been looking forward to for months—ever since she picked out the tile for the bathroom floors. Plus, it was her first time laying tile. No matter how many books she read or videos she watched, nothing compared to doing it herself.

Daisy mixed the bucket of mortar using the special attachment for the drill. Lance showed her how to spread it on the floor and the tile, and the small thrill of achievement rippled through her as Daisy pressed the first tile in the corner.

The real victory would come when the floor was complete, but she couldn't hide her satisfied grin.

Lance gave one in return, his teeth flashing briefly before he spoke, "Great job. Now only one hundred more to go."

Daisy replied with her typical can-do attitude, but three hours later the drudgery of repetition had sucked away her enthusiasm. "Remind me again why I want to do all the work myself," she said to Lance as he dumped yet another bag of mortar into the bucket.

He looked up at her, "Actually, I'm not sure you ever told me."

Unsure how to respond, Daisy continued spreading the mortar. The sensation of being watched made her neck itch, and she turned to find Lance staring at her with a raised eyebrow instead of heading out to make the next cut. "What?"

He laughed, "Why do you insist on learning all this?"

Daisy ducked her head. "I don't know. This place is my dream and I didn't want to leave it in the hands of anyone else. Besides, I think I needed to prove to myself that I could do it." Heat rose in her cheeks, but with Lance's kind eyes watching hers carefully, she couldn't help but explain the rest. "I came back home after New York with no real sense of direction. It just felt like everyone else had their thing, and I tried everything hoping to find mine. But since I couldn't dance anymore, nothing felt right. One night, I couldn't sleep and I ended up watching This Renovation House reruns. I was totally hooked!" She laughed and looked at the mortar dried on her jeans and the knee pads she wore. "I know it's not exactly glamorous, but I fell in love with the idea of taking this old, wornout shell of a house and making it new again."

Lance was nodding along and, for maybe the first time, Daisy felt they had something in common. She continued, "It feels significant to be doing it with my own hands, though." She gave a half-hearted chuckle, "I'm sorry it makes your life more difficult."

"I don't mind," Lance said softly. "I had my dad to teach me all of this stuff. I went with him on jobs and worked as his assistant." Lance smiled, "I can't imagine having a five-year-old trying to help lay tile." Daisy struggled to wipe up a dollop of mortar from the top of a freshly laid tile and he chuckled, "Well, maybe I have a little idea."

Daisy rolled her eyes at the comment, laughing. "Your dad has taught me a lot, even if I still have so much to learn," she acknowledged.

"I've been doing this for ten years and I'm still learning. The best way to learn is exactly what you are doing—getting your hands dirty and learning along the way." He shook his head. "I don't think I be doing this without my dad's influence. I love it like he did though, for many of the same reasons as you." He hesitated and Daisy held her breath, hoping he would say more. "There is something amazing about building from the ground up. But it is even more magical to take something ugly and damaged and make it new and beautiful."

Daisy looked up thoughtfully, "Those are my favorite verses in the Bible. The Old Testament promises from God where he talks about making all things new and renovating hearts of stone."

"Exactly. God is a Creator and a Restorer." When Lance spoke confidently about God's character, Daisy felt her resistance crack. "And we are made in his image. Our desire to build or to see the damaged things renewed comes from the image of God in us. I think it's incredible."

Daisy had never thought of it that way. Her desire to create beauty was the reflection of God's character. God who embodies all beauty and creativity had instilled that desire in her.

"Wow," she said. Who knew Lance was so poetic? It was obvious his love of the Lord impacted everything he did. Another mark in his favor. Daisy better be careful, because her mental list of admirable qualities was slowly overtaking the list of negatives.

"But," Lance said, giving the bucket a tap with his hand, "sometimes it's just a house and a bathroom floor that needs done before the mortar dries out."

THE ONLY CASUALTY of the bathroom tile project was a five-gallon bucket. Daisy sent him home and said she would clean up, but Lance came back the next day to find the mortar dried solid. He wouldn't make that mistake again. His irritation was short-lived though, because Daisy's fresh perspective and appreciation of even the smallest tasks was reminding him why he loved renovations.

It surprised him how much he enjoyed working with Daisy. Her infectious enthusiasm and laughter were hard to resist. Never a dull moment.

Today, they would install the vanity cabinets in both bathrooms. Lance wandered through the living room, where he had set up his own base of operations. He rifled around the folding table, lifting stacks of papers and shuffling boxes to find his cordless drill.

"Daisy?" he yelled up the stairs.

Footsteps thumped on the wooden staircase and Daisy poked her head around the corner, "What's up?"

"Have you seen my drill?" Lance was trying to keep the agitation out of his voice. Every time he was looking for something, it was nowhere near the place he left it. How hard was it to put things back where you got them? Or to clean up at the end of the day and put things into a semblance of order?

Daisy was thinking and with every second, Lance felt his irritation rise. "It might be upstairs? Or maybe I was using it for the curtains in the dining room?" Daisy shrugged, and her complete nonchalance was the last straw.

"You can't just move all my stuff and not put it back, Daisy!" Her eyes grew wide and Lance knew he was yelling, but couldn't help it. "I know you'd prefer to work and live in chaos at all times. Some of us actually like to be able to find things when we look for them, or know the battery will be charged when we need it."

"I'm sorry, but I—"

"Stop! You can't apologize and make excuses at the same time. Just..." Lance clinched his jaw and pulled his hat off with a quick motion, slapping it against his thigh in frustration. Before he could yell at Daisy anymore, Lance stormed out the front door, letting the door slam behind him.

On one hand, it wasn't a big deal. He didn't mind if Daisy borrowed his drill to get things done. His was more powerful and had a better battery life than the basic driver she'd picked up. But Daisy didn't respect his things or the worksite organization. It drove him crazy. It was one thing for her to leave her own tools strewn about. It was another for her to leave his tools where he couldn't find them.

The woman was a basket case! It never even crossed Daisy's mind to pick up or throw something in a trash can instead of in the corner of the room.

After a quick lap around the house, Lance walked through the back door and found his drill on a windowsill in the dining room. Apparently, Designer Daisy had hung curtains last night. It wasn't on the current project to-do list, but Lance realized Daisy liked to find bite-sized jobs she could tackle independently. At least she was gaining some perspective on what type of jobs those were.

Hanging curtains? Sure.

Pulling cable through the attic for new lights? The memory of their first meeting came to mind and he smiled.

Daisy Bloom was giving him more gray hairs than any client before. It didn't help that he found it so hard to stay mad at her. Already, he'd forgiven Messy Jessie for misplacing his drill, and she hadn't really apologized. Perhaps even crazier—he knew it wouldn't be the last time.

Why was he so drawn to her? They were too different, and her world of chaos and disorder was like nails on a chalkboard to his natural sense of organization and desire for predictability.

When they worked side-by-side on a project, it was flawless. Daisy seemed to anticipate his needs, offering a tool or suggestion before he even thought to request it. Even Cody, who'd been on his team almost since the beginning, didn't work with him as seamlessly. Of course, Cody didn't misplace the screws he was holding for two minutes or measure a board an inch short. But Daisy found creative solutions to problems, often suggesting an easier way to tackle something when Lance was crashing ahead with the same old tactic he'd always used.

All in all, she was an asset. Not that he would tell her. It would go straight to her head, and he'd probably show up to find her waist deep in a pile of rubble where she'd tried to take down the chimney herself.

Ten minutes later, Lance sent Daisy to the hardware store for a tube of caulk for the bathroom vanity, hoping by the time she returned, he could apologize for his outburst. He was under the sink, wrangling the flexible piping into place when heavy footsteps sounded next to him. Lance craned his neck to look out of the cabinet, expecting Daisy's impossibly small work boots. Instead, he saw well-worn boots belonging to someone with far larger feet.

Lance frowned and extracted his frame from the tight space under the bathroom sink. An open hand, weathered and creased with dirt, reached down and Lance took it, pulling himself up as a loud voice greeted him, "You must be Lance."

The eyes that met Lance's were bright and inviting, as though perpetually filled with laughter. Eyes exactly the same gray-green color as Daisy's and the man's salt-and-pepper hair could mean only one thing. This was Mr. Bloom, Daisy and Hawthorne's father. "Lance Matthews, sir." Lance took the hand again and shook it firmly.

"Nice to meet you, Lance. I'm Keith," he said, confirming Lance's assumption.

"Daisy ran to the hardware store," Lance explained.

Keith waved a hand, "I saw her car was gone. But

your truck was still here, so I figured I would come say hello."

Lance nodded. "Have you seen much of the work we've done?"

Lance walked Daisy's father around the house, pointing out projects they'd done recently. Keith's eyebrows wiggled as he said, "It's neater in here than I would expect from my daughter."

Covering his laugh with a cough, Lance nodded. "Yes sir, she is a bit disorganized. But we are making it work."

Keith hummed, flipping the new light switch in the north bedroom. "So, I've heard. Daisy can't seem to stop talking about Lance this and Lance that." His cheeks grew hot. Keith continued, "From her attitude, I half-expected to find out Lance Matthews had horns and a tail."

Lance scoffed, "Leave it to Daisy to equate cleanliness with untold evil." She was complaining to her family about him? Was he really that bad?

Keith laughed heartily, his deep voice booming through the empty room. "Oh, it's not quite that bad. If I know Daisy, which I think I do, she's exaggerating her own frustration. Probably to throw off her sisters who can't seem to leave her alone about you.

Any idea why they would be goading her?" Keith gave him a questioning glance.

Lance's eyebrows shot upward. He had no idea why Daisy's sisters would be teasing. He was just the contractor. And other than the crazy intense desire to kiss Daisy after seeing her dance, nothing had happened. Nothing would happen.

Now to convince her father of the same. "Well, Mr. Bloom, I'm not—".

"Call me Keith." They walked down the stairs to see the rest of the house.

Lance rubbed a forearm under his baseball cap and nodded. "Okay, Keith. I can't say I have any idea. Of course, I never had siblings myself. But I can assure you I am nothing to Daisy except a thorn in her side pushing her to finish this project."

Keith pressed his lips together and tipped his head.

They stepped into the kitchen, and Daisy's car pulled up in front of the house. Keith glanced at his daughter and turned back to Lance and said, "It was a pleasure to meet you, Lance. You take care of my girl, okay?"

"I'll make sure she doesn't hurt herself." Lance responded safely.

Keith's eyes seemed to see straight through

Lance, at the conflicted interest and doubts inside. "I'm not so worried about her hurting herself. But I have faith in you; you're good for Daisy."

Lance struggled to come up with a response. What should he say to that cryptic remark? Maybe Keith was talking about his help on the project. Before Lance could comment about how Daisy was quite capable on her own, the door swung open and Keith crossed to greet his daughter with a bear hug before making excuses and ducking outside.

The exchange between father and daughter made him smile. Daisy was a lucky woman to have the family she did. When her father was gone, Daisy looked at him and held up a brown paper bag from a fast-food joint. A peace offering in the form of a greasy hamburger—his favorite kind.

9

*B*lood pressure rising, Daisy stood on the step in an effort to gain some high ground. She and Lance had been going around for twenty minutes about the kitchen plans.

"Just because you have numbers and spread-sheets doesn't mean you are right about this. Where is your vision?" She threw up her arms in frustration.

"Vision won't matter if you go out of business, Daisy. Think about how many reservations it would take to pay for the stove you want!" She didn't want to think about that. If the food was incredible, the stove would be worth it and the reservations would come.

Daisy had researched, and the most important things for a bed-and-breakfast were comfortable beds, a picture-perfect setting, and the best breakfast the guests had ever had. Not necessarily in that order. Lance might be the expert when it came to construction, but this was her dream.

The front door slammed, but Daisy was too fired up to care and yelled at Lance, "I'm the owner of this house, and I will make the decisions here!" She didn't play the boss card very often, but this kitchen needed to be something special. What else would attract a brilliant chef to a small bed-and-breakfast in the middle of nowhere?

From the corner of her eye, she saw Hawthorne peer around the doorway with hands raised in surrender. "I come in peace."

Immediately, Lance turned to him, gesturing wildly with a tape measure. "Tell your sister it is crazy to have a commercial size refrigerator and stove for a bed-and-breakfast that will serve eight people one meal a day!"

Daisy stomped her foot, her nose sprinkled with drywall dust. "Tell Lance I'm not paying him to criticize my plans." She glared at Hawthorne with her hand on her hip.

Lance sputtered and Hawthorne held up a hand. "Whoa, whoa, whoa. Take a minute, you two." He shook his head. "I don't know what's going on here; I could have sworn you were finally getting along."

Daisy ducked her head. They were getting along. Except when Lance had freaked out about her borrowing his tools. What was the big deal anyway? They'd gotten so much work done, it still surprised her. He was superefficient—which was a blessing and a curse. She loved the progress, but she was not enjoying the process. Every day, Lance knew exactly what they should be working on. And even if she didn't feel like working on that particular project that day, it was what they did. Because Lance was always right. Except this time. When it came to the kitchen, Daisy was right and she was not backing down.

Hawthorne looked at Lance and asked for his opinion, which made Daisy's eyes widen further. Just like a man to take a man's side. Daisy tried to protest, but her brother held up a finger to silence her. "Let the man talk, Daze."

Daisy crossed her arms and gave her brother a dirty look. She'd let him talk, but then she'd let him have a piece of her mind.

Lance explained his ridiculous argument that the commercial kitchen would cost too much and when Daisy was finally given the chance to talk, she spoke quickly.

"This bed-and-breakfast is going to be top notch and I need to have the best chef I can reasonably afford. I'm not going to cheap out on the kitchen and scare away the talent! A world-class chef deserves a world-class kitchen."

She finally lost steam and waited for Hawthorne to speak, refusing to look at Lance. Hawthorne waved a thumb toward Daisy. "I'm with her on this one." Victory! Daisy jumped up and pointed triumphantly at her contractor before Hawthorne interrupted her celebration, "Not for the reasons you said, sis."

She paused mid-fist pump.

This was an unexpected twist. It wasn't like Hawthorne to offer ideas or really do anything beyond the bare minimum. Another side of her brother emerged as Daisy listened to him share how the kitchen in the bed-and-breakfast could operate as the culinary center of the farm, a space for catering prep for events at Storybook Barn and even for Poppy's organic canned foods business to expand.

It made sense, Daisy had to admit. The only argument Lance made that almost convinced her he could be right was the kitchen would only be used for a few hours each day. It did seem like a waste of space, but it was a bed-and-breakfast. With

Hawthorne's idea, the kitchen could be utilized more often and be an investment that benefited everyone. Lily would love to be able to pull catering inside and offer it to her brides, and Poppy hated having to use the kitchen at the main house.

Daisy glanced at Lance and he nodded to Hawthorne, "That makes sense," he conceded. He turned to Daisy and gave a charming smirk. "You win." She grinned in response and he added, "On a technicality." Their anger had evaporated and his smile was almost flirtatious.

"I'll take it," Daisy said before floating up the stairs to call Mandy. She had to make sure everything was in place for Mandy's bachelorette party and the wedding this weekend. The important thing was she would get the amazing kitchen she'd dreamed of. Well, the amazing kitchen and the fact that Lance had been wrong.

10

*S*ince Hawthorne helped settle the debate, Lance and Daisy planned the kitchen, with the big commercial appliances she insisted on. The challenge now was making the kitchen still seem homey and inviting, since it would be visible to guests. Plus, when there were no guests, Daisy would still live here. Wouldn't she? He hadn't asked her.

Would Hawthorne still live here? Either way, it was none of his business. Things had been tense around the house lately. Since his big blowup about the tools, Daisy had lost a bit of her spark, and he hated knowing it was his fault. The good news was she'd been leaving his tools alone.

Today, they were hanging cabinets and open shelving on one wall and installing the large center island. They didn't have a cabinet jack for the upper cabinets, which is why Lance found himself crouched under a cabinet, bracing it on his shoulders. Daisy perched on a step stool in front of him, screwing the cabinet into the wall. Far too slowly, if the cramp near his shoulder blade was any indication.

She said something, but it was muffled by the cabinet between them.

"I can't hear you," he reminded her with a slight eye roll. Daisy had tried to make conversation while she was supposed to be inserting screws half a dozen times.

Lance tested the cabinet by reducing the weight he was supporting, eventually ducking out entirely. To release the tension from being curled up for so long, Lance rolled his shoulders and stretched his neck muscles.

"I said, how is your dad doing?" Daisy repeated with a slight smile.

Lance felt the tug on his heart at her thoughtfulness. "He's doing really well. Actually up and walking around already. He says he hates physical therapy but that his therapist is nice," Lance said with a chuckle.

Daisy grinned, "That's great. I've been meaning

find time to visit him. I need to catch him up on everything around here." Her face fell and she continued, "Oh, I'm sure you've probably told him everything anyway."

Shaking his head, Lance explained that his dad had forbidden Lance from talking about the project. Greg said he wanted to hear it from Daisy or see it with his own eyes. Of course, the ban on Bloom's Farm conversation happened one day when Greg was tired of hearing Lance complain about Daisy, but she didn't need to know that.

She brightened, "That's so sweet. I'll call him later today and set up a time. I'm sure your mom would appreciate a little notice before a visitor drops in."

A pang of sadness cut through him at her assumption. Of course Daisy would think his family was perfect, like hers. "Actually, my mom split when I was a toddler. Too much to handle, I guess," he joked. Unwilling to see the pity in her eyes, he started counting out screws for the next cabinet. "It's been my dad and me ever since."

Delicate fingertips grazed his arm, and he felt the heat of her touch sink into his bones as she patted his arm. "I'm so sorry, Lance. I didn't know."

Why did people apologize for things that were

out of their control? It wasn't like Daisy had scared away his mother—that had been him.

As though she could read his thoughts, Daisy said, "It's her loss. You and your dad..." Daisy paused, her eyes meeting his. "You're good men," she finished. Heat crawled up Lance's neck at the praise and he tried to rub it away with a squeeze of his hand.

"It's fine. It was a long time ago. And Dad really was the best. He never acted like I was a burden, even when it meant bringing me along to work or leaving a job early to come to my basketball games." Lance still didn't know how his dad had done it. Single parents were superheroes in his mind. Now that he was considering the possibility of settling down, if he ever found the right woman, he knew he didn't want to make the same mistake as his father. Lance would never marry someone who would follow a whim and leave all their obligations behind. He wanted someone grounded and responsible —like him.

Daisy's blond ponytail swished as she walked across the kitchen, retrieving a can of soda like she'd done several times every day since they started working together. Suddenly, a bottle of water came flying at him, and he caught it an instant before it bounced off his stomach.

The distinctive pop and fizz of Daisy's soda opening filled the kitchen, and he looked up from the bottle in his hands. Daisy shrugged and said, "I figured since all you ever drink is water, I'd better have some on hand for you."

He twisted the cap off and raised the bottle in a salute. "Thanks."

The silence stretched and Daisy flicked a fingernail on the top of the soda can, a metallic twang sounding. "I can't imagine being an only child," Daisy mused.

Lance exhaled a quiet chuckle. "I can't imagine having so many siblings. How many of you are there, again?"

Daisy listed her siblings on her fingers. "Lily, Hawthorne, Poppy, Lavender, and Rose. And of course, me and my twin sister, Andi."

"Andi? Doesn't she get a flower name?" Lance asked. It didn't escape him that the Bloom family had really embraced their last name.

A mischievous smile flashed on Daisy's face. "Oh, she definitely does—but she hates it." Daisy looked around the space, as though to make sure her sister hadn't somehow snuck up on her. "Andi's actual name is Dandelion."

With the inhale following Daisy's pronouncement, water caught in Lance's throat and he coughed. "Dandelion? Seriously?"

A spark of laughter danced in Daisy's eyes, beckoning him from across the room, "I know. I'm so glad I lucked out on that one. If I'd been born seven minutes sooner, I would be Dandelion."

Lance shook his head, "Poor girl."

Daisy waved her hand, "She's over it now. But definitely don't call her Dandelion to her face, or you'll be sorry."

The somber warning was out of character for Daisy, and Lance couldn't tell if she was pulling his chain. When he asked for confirmation, she explained that Andi was an expert in hand-to-hand combat and was just as likely to knock Lance to the ground as give him a hug.

"She really doesn't like to be called Dandelion." Daisy said, her mouth tucked beside her hand as though she was sharing national secrets.

They shared a grin and Lance replied, "I can't really blame her. It must be hard to have her so far away."

Daisy stared into the depths of her Diet Dr. Pepper and replied soberly, "Yeah, it is. I have Poppy and the others, but it isn't the same. Andi is... my best friend, I guess." Finally, she looked up at him with a smile. "My mom used to say we might as well have been conjoined, because we were always together. Then Andi signed up for the Army and everything changed."

His lack of siblings meant Lance couldn't really understand, but the idea of being so far away from his dad was similar. "People always ask me if I would ever leave Greencastle, but it's where Dad is. I don't think I could do it. It's always been me and him. A team."

Daisy nodded. "Yeah, I thought that's what Andi and I were like. But she left after I got back from New York anyway and I sort of... drifted for a while." Lance hated the sadness in her voice and turned Daisy's attention to the one thing he knew would bring a smile to her face.

"And then you had the idea to open a bed-and-breakfast?"

Daisy sipped and nodded. "It took a few years of working other places on the farm before I was ready. But living here, you drive past this run-down house every day. It seemed like the natural thing to do."

Lance looked around the kitchen and responded.

"I'm glad you are giving her new life. It would be a shame for a house like this to go to waste."

Daisy smiled and Lance felt ten feet tall, knowing he had been the one to replace her frown. "At least that's one thing we can agree on," she quipped, and his lips twitched at her teasing tone.

"Come on, we've got two more cabinets to hang before we call it a day."

11

*C*rawlspaces were the worst invention of all time. All things considered, the space under this hundred-year-old house was relatively clean. Still, having to crawl on the dirt under a house to access plumbing was a terrible strategy. Daisy and Lance were installing a new drain line for the kitchen sink, since it was being repositioned. Plumbers did not earn enough money.

Positioned by Lance's waist, Daisy couldn't quite see what he was doing behind the beam extending into the ground and holding up this portion of the house. He reached back and handed her a section of pipe. Ancient pipe, apparently.

The new sink was only three feet away from the

previous location, but it still meant cutting into the drain and running a new line to the island.

Which meant laying here in the dirt next to Lance. The slightly musty air in the crawlspace was surprisingly warm, given the brisk fall temperature outside. Much to Daisy's relief, they'd encountered no animals—living or dead—in the space.

It was hard not to notice Lance's strong legs and smooth torso when he was lying on his stomach, with his legs extended beside her. The overwhelming urge to untuck his T-shirt would have to be ignored, but Daisy constantly wanted to do whatever she could to mess with Lance's desire for perfection and order.

Lately, she found herself intentionally leaving one screw short of fully tightened, just to watch him notice and finish the task himself. Last week, she had written a list of projects, but left some uncrossed off that they had already finished.

This morning, Daisy brought down the wrong diameter pipe for the drain. Actually, that hadn't been intentional, but Lance was certainly irritated. Which didn't make any sense, because she was the one who had to inch out of the crawlspace to get the correct pipe from his truck. All he had to do was wait.

Now it was Daisy's turn to wait, and patience

was not her strong suit. Wanting to see the action, Daisy attempted to scoot herself closer to the drain. The beam was making it nearly impossible, along with the restricted head room.

Still, she hadn't taken on this project to sit on the sidelines, and Daisy laid alongside Lance, sneaking in beside him so she could see his face and hands.

With a grunt, Lance shifted slightly, giving her an additional inch of space. Of course, it didn't prevent the warm pressure of his leg against hers, or her hip bumping his as he twisted the pipe into place.

Focus deserted her and she stared blankly toward his hands and the flexing muscles beneath the sleeve of his T-shirt, comprehending nothing beyond his presence.

"Hand me that zip tie," Lance said, jolting Daisy from her reverie.

His finger pointed next to her shoulder, and she fumbled for the plastic strap. While Lance expertly secured the new drain along the floor joist, a bead of sweat made its way from his temple to his jaw, and Daisy traced the path with her eyes.

"Sorry it's so tight down here. I'm sure you didn't get to see much," Lance said with a glance in her direction. "Can you scoot up a little more and I can talk you through it?"

Apparently, Lance was not nearly as affected by her physical presence as she was by his, so Daisy inched her way forward until they were eye to eye. Lance rolled over onto his back, and Daisy did the same. A maze of clean white pipes crisscrossed under the floor above her and Lance began to talk.

He pointed out the old drain, where he'd spliced into it, and the new sink location, with water supply and drain line newly rerouted. Daisy nodded along and watched his hands as they danced through the air above their heads while the cool ground anchored her. The headlamp strapped to Lance's baseball hat lit the underside of the floor and the features above them as he explained.

Daisy turned slightly, her eyes finding his face, the side visible in the shadow of his cap. "Thank you."

Lance's hands fell. One brushed her hip, and he turned his head toward her with a small smile, blinding her with the light for a moment before he clicked it off, leaving only her handheld flashlight casting inky shadows between them. "No problem. I figure if you went to all the trouble of coming down here, you might as well know what we did."

"What you did," she corrected.

Lance shrugged his shoulders and offered, "I'm happy to take it all apart so you can do it over again."

Daisy laughed, the sound bouncing gaily in the tight space. "That's okay, I'm good."

A short chuckle from Lance and he propped himself up on one elbow, still looking at her. Feeling vulnerable, Daisy quickly mirrored his position.

"Daisy, I—"

"I hope you—"

Their words overlapped, cutting each other off. Lance gestured for her to go. Feeling self-conscious, but also comforted by their close quarters, Daisy spoke quietly. "I'm just really grateful for everything you've done here. I know I'm not the easiest person to work for and that you could probably make more money with fewer headaches elsewhere. I don't know if it's just because of your dad or what, but—" His fingertips tipped her chin up and the contact made the words die on her lips.

"I'm glad I'm here, Daisy." Lance's words soothed the bruises Daisy didn't know she carried from others who'd mocked her as too difficult.

"Really?" she asked, studying his face for clues. Was he lying? Simply telling her the words she wanted to hear?

"Really," Lance confirmed. Then he sighed and released her chin and tipped his head back. "At first, it was just because of the house. I've always wanted to work on a historic house like this, but haven't had the opportunity. But now," he looked back and Daisy swore he would be able to hear her heart beat across the small space, "I think you are pretty special, Daisy. How could I not be impressed with a woman willing to lay tile and brave the crawlspace?"

Daisy bit her lip to keep the smile from overtaking her face.

"I'm serious. Don't get me wrong, you still drive me crazy with your singing and chaos and empty soda cans," Daisy gave an embarrassed smile, but Lance continued, "but you are also kind and determined." He paused, studied her face and angled his shoulders toward hers. "And beautiful," he added before reaching his hand to the nape of her neck. Daisy's eyes fell closed and she felt his hesitation just before his lips descended on hers.

It should have been awkward, elbows propped on the dry dirt and their bodies angled awkwardly to avoid the support beam. In the moment though, everything beyond Lance and his kiss disappeared from Daisy's thoughts. Surprisingly soft and full lips melded with hers, gently at first, and then with more fervor.

Too soon, the kiss ended, leaving Daisy a speechless mess of nerve endings. She felt like she might have turned into a giant pile of ooze that would have to be dragged out of the crawlspace. Or sucked up with the shop vac.

When she finally opened her eyes, Lance was still impossibly close. The pressure of his legs against the length of hers was impossible to ignore and Daisy squirmed, desperate to create space between them, but there was none to be found in the confines of the shadowy crawlspace.

"Daisy—" his hoarse whisper sent tingles of electricity through her entire body.

"We shouldn't do this," she said, her voice a whisper to match his. "We aren't the same."

"Maybe that's a good thing," he protested.

She knew that wasn't true. They were too different. They worked well together, and the physical spark was definitely alive and well, if that kiss was any indication. But there was no way a long-term relationship would work.

Daisy would drive him crazy, and trying to please him would mean hiding parts of herself that she cherished. Still, even knowing the future wasn't an option, she wasn't ready to say goodbye to the moment.

Thoughts flickered across Daisy's face like words on a typewriter. Her mind was made up, but Lance hadn't been joking. Maybe their differences were what made them such good partners. Wouldn't it be the same in life?

Daisy raised her chin and shook her head. "I'm sorry, Lance."

She leaned forward, as much as the cramped space would allow, and pressed her lips to his. Shock flooded his system, but he recovered quickly and pulled her close, deepening the kiss and trying his best to convey what he had obviously failed to do with words: they fit together, despite their differences.

How could she say sorry and then kiss him like this? Only seconds later, the warmth of the kiss was replaced by empty space as Daisy broke the connection and quickly slid out of his reach, retreating to the entrance of the crawlspace.

His breath sounded deafening in the enclosed space, and his heartbeat thundered hard against his chest. With a deep sigh, Lance laid his head back on the cold ground. He hadn't figured Daisy for a coward, but she'd run away from him.

Was she right? Was Lance just caught up in the romance of—he looked around in the dark—the crawlspace? His quiet laughter echoed back to him. Not exactly champagne and strawberries.

What had he been thinking, coming onto her like that? When Daisy revealed the depth of character behind her scatterbrained tendencies, he couldn't help but be drawn to her. She was so full of life and joy, and Lance wanted to capture it for himself.

There was a list of characteristics for his future wife that Lance had made once in youth group. Disorganized and addicted to Diet Dr. Pepper had definitely not been on the list. Daisy loved old houses, her family, and the Lord. Why couldn't that be enough?

Daisy was right, they were complete opposites. But somehow, he wanted to be with her anyway. It wasn't logical, which was pretty much his entire decision-making process. Something about Daisy made him feel a million things all at once. She made him want to throw all of his caution and lists out the window. He needed to be rational. Thinking things through and being careful was how he'd built everything he had. Lance couldn't change for her. Daisy was probably up there right now, starting a project they weren't ready for. Which meant it was time for him to get out of here and prevent any mishaps Daisy might get into.

While he was at it, Lance would tell her she was right. There was no use in pursuing a relationship that had no future. Even if kissing her while cooped up in a dingy crawlspace was better than all his previous life kisses combined.

12

*D*aisy fidgeted with the loose screws on the table trying to forget what just happened in the crawl space. That kiss! Her few dates in college never involved kisses like that. Her cheeks flamed with the memory of her boldness. What had she been thinking, declaring their complete incompatibility and then kissing him before wiggling her way out of the crawl space?

Her heart jumped when the door opened, figuring it was Lance coming to work out whatever had just happened. Instead, her sister looked wide-eyed around the kitchen.

"Wow, this is incredible, Daze," Lavender said softly as she admired the white granite countertops and cabinets with open shelves of raw edge wood.

Daisy couldn't help but smile. Her vision for the kitchen was coming together, and she'd done much of it with her own two hands.

"Thanks, you should see the upstairs."

"Maybe another day. Right now, I have something I need to talk to you about. Do you have a minute?"

It was unlike Lavender to be so serious, and concern immediately flooded Daisy. A thousand possible explanations ran through her mind. Was Lavender in trouble?

"Yeah, now is fine." Movement in the entryway caught her eye as Lance stepped through the front door. He stopped in the doorway of the kitchen, his eyes moving to Lavender before meeting Daisy's. Daisy gave him a tight smile and tried to convey with her eyes that they could talk later. Right now, she needed to hear what Lavender had to say. Lance turned and went upstairs, and Daisy turned back to the small bistro table. It was still the only real seating in the house, not counting the folding camp chairs in the makeshift living room.

Impatiently, Daisy remained silent and waited for her younger sister to speak.

Lavender pulled her phone from the concealed pocket of her skirt and set it on the table before looking up at Daisy. "So, I've been working on setting up the online infrastructure for the B&B."

"Okay?" Confusion filled Daisy's voice. That sounded exciting, why was Lavender so subdued?

"I've got the website ready except for the final pictures of the common areas and guest rooms. And pricing. But, I set up the Facebook page and instead of keeping it private, I accidentally made it live." Lavender grabbed the phone. "More and more, websites are pulling reviews from other sites and compiling them in one place. Which is great, because your good reviews are shown no matter where someone looks. But it also means your bad reviews are, too."

What on earth was Lovey talking about? The bed-and-breakfast couldn't have reviews, it wasn't even open yet. When she asked, Lavender sighed and thumbed her phone until she found the page she wanted.

Bloom's Farm Bed and Breakfast. "Seven total reviews? Two stars!" Daisy read. "How do we even have reviews? Reservations aren't open yet."

Lavender shook her head, "I don't know what's going on, but Facebook pages can have reviews from anyone. And someone has decided to attack your bed-and-breakfast. Each of the reviews is unique enough that I can't say they are from one person, and the website seems to agree, because Facebook won't remove the reviews."

Daisy's head was spinning. Who on earth would lie about her bed-and-breakfast? Why would they care?

"What happens if you just delete the page?" Daisy asked. Maybe they could start over in a few months and the whole thing would blow over.

"That's the bad part. These reviews have already been picked up by a dozen other travel sites. If someone searches for Bloom's Farm Bed and Breakfast, they see terrible reviews plastered all over the web. I also found message boards with posts where someone bashed us for obviously fake things, like the bathrooms being filthy and the property being run down. It's just a whole fiasco."

Daisy's heart settled deep into the pit of her stomach. How could she battle an unknown enemy? What were her options?

"What do you think we should do?" she asked Lavender.

"If it was just one or two things, I would think it was a mistake, like another property somewhere and people got confused. But it is definitely targeted. One of the message boards even mentions Storybook

Barn." Daisy groaned and Lavender laid her hand on Daisy's arm. "If there is one thing I know, it is the internet. I've been studying how hotels respond to bad reviews, and I think our best bet is to continue what we are doing, make sure we take stellar pictures of the space, and respond to each review politely pointing out they must have the wrong hotel, because this one isn't open yet."

Daisy nodded along as Lavender continued, "As soon as we are open and the real reviews start rolling in, it will be obvious that these were lies. Plus, with our own social media ads and posts, we can drown out the negative stuff with our own messaging."

It didn't seem like enough, but at this point, there was nothing else Daisy could do. The plan didn't change just because some mystery person didn't like it.

Daisy stared at the phone. Two stars. "Okay, go ahead and do that. If you want, you can start taking some pictures of the finished spaces. We've still got work here in the kitchen and I have to redo the blue bathroom upstairs. But since the new ones are done, Hawthorne and I can start using them."

Lavender could work on the internet side of things. Daisy was going to figure out who had it out for her, because they had underestimated who they were messing with. Her dreams didn't die so easily. And unlike her dream of dancing, this bed-and-breakfast would not be derailed.

"Okay, that's fine. We just move forward." Lavender squeezed her hand again.

"I'm trusting you here, Lovey. Are you sure I can't get on there and reply to each review with an angry rant about their lies?" Lavender laughed at Daisy's question, but Daisy hadn't exactly been joking. She wanted to get mad.

It was probably a good thing Lavender had been the one to see the comments first; she was much more deliberate and level-headed. They walked through the kitchen and toward the staircase. Daisy gestured up the stairs, "Come on upstairs and I'll show you what Lance and I have finished so far."

After the short tour, Daisy found Lance ripping down tile in the blue bathroom. Interesting, because this job wasn't next on his precious list. His forearms rippled with the weight of the sledgehammer and she couldn't help but remember what it felt like to be pulled close to him under the house.

Daisy leaned against the doorframe, "Hey."

Lance paused, his breathing heavy. His jaw flexed, "Hey."

"Apparently, someone is trying to sink the bed-

and-breakfast before it's even open. I've got a slew of negative reviews."

Lance frowned and set down the sledgehammer, "I'm sorry, Daisy."

She shrugged. She hadn't sought him out to talk about the reviews. "About the crawlspace..."

Lance held up a hand. "It's okay. You're probably right."

Daisy raised her eyebrows at his admission. "Can I get that in writing?" she joked.

Lance smiled, but it didn't reach his eyes. His gaze met hers and he said, "I'm not sorry about what happened down there, but I agree it wouldn't be... wise to pursue something more."

For some reason, disappointment settled in her stomach. Even though Daisy had been the one to declare their incompatibility, it was strangely painful to realize they wouldn't share secret kisses and flirtatious glances anymore.

"Just friends, then?" she confirmed.

"Friends," he responded with a sharp nod. Then, as though he needed to hit something, Lance picked up the sledgehammer and swung it at the plaster wall. Daisy backed out of the bathroom slowly. Space would be good. She and Lance would be back to normal before long.

Daisy had tried to talk to Andi that weekend, but hadn't been able to connect. On Monday, Andi sent a cryptic email about being busy. So, Tuesday afternoon, Daisy wandered up to the main house after Lance left for the day and found her mother making pies. Thanksgiving was fast approaching, and the holiday would be a welcome break from strained conversations with Lance.

Maybe a pie-crust cookie would make her feel better. Daisy had been in a funk ever since Lavender told her about the online bashing of the inn.

It was hard to be enthusiastic when opposition popped out of the woodwork. It wasn't the end of the world, but Daisy couldn't help but obsess about it.

"Have you seen Poppy?" she asked her mom.

"I think she is around here somewhere. She's been kind of scattered lately."

"Yeah," Daisy agreed, "I feel like I have hardly seen her." She left her mom to her baking and looked for Poppy in her room, with no luck.

In the pole-barn, Daisy found Poppy talking in hushed tones on her cellphone. Poppy glanced up as she approached and quickly ended the call. Her sister flashed a broad smile, but it looked forced and Daisy frowned back.

"Who was that?" she asked.

Poppy replied, "Who was who?" with a wide-eyed look of innocence.

With a raised eyebrow, Daisy replied. "Whatever, don't tell me. But don't think we don't all know something is going on with you."

"I don't—"

"It's fine," Daisy held up a hand. "You don't have to tell me. But you should talk to someone. And you know I'm here for you if you need me, right?"

Poppy nodded. "Thanks. It's just a bit... complicated right now."

Daisy coughed a laugh and said, "Tell me about it. I've got cyber bullies and crawlspace kisses. Plus, Hawthorne is being all weird and responsible."

"Whoa, whoa, whoa. Crawlspace kisses?" Poppy pushed Daisy over to a bench against the wall of the barn. "I'm going to need a bit more information on that."

"Oh, sure. I'm just supposed to spill my guts to you while you keep all your secrets?" Daisy pressed her lips shut and mimed locking them with her fingers.

Poppy rolled her eyes, "Come on, Daze. You came here to talk about this."

"Maybe I did. But you've got to give me something! Just one tidbit." Daisy flashed the pouty, begging expression that had helped her get her way so many times over the years.

Poppy sighed and gave a sheepish smile, "It's Harrison."

Daisy's mouth dropped open in shock, "Like, your Harrison? Harrison Coulter?"

Eyes squeezed shut, Poppy nodded quickly. She opened one eye to gauge Daisy's reaction.

"Oh my." Harrison Coulter was a name she hadn't heard Poppy say in ages. "What did he want?"

Poppy shook her head, "That's all I can tell you right now."

"Are you kidding me? That's the biggest tease!" Daisy pushed a hand against her sister's shoulder.

Poppy smiled. "I don't know... Crawlspace kisses is a pretty big teaser, too, Daze." She gave a pointed look and Daisy felt herself blush.

"Okay, fine. Maybe." Now that Daisy had found her sister, she didn't know what she wanted to share. "Lance kissed me in the crawlspace." Poppy wrinkled her nose and Daisy had to laugh, "I know, it sounds super bizarre, but it actually wasn't weird at all. Well, other than the fact that it was Lance and we are completely wrong for each other."

Leaning in intently, Poppy asked, "So what did you do?

"Well, I told him we were completely wrong for each other." She groaned at the memory and tipped her head back against the wall. "Then I kissed him again." At Poppy's gasp, she delivered the kicker, "And then I ran away. Or crawled away, anyway."

Poppy's laughter filled their small corner of the barn and eventually Daisy joined in.

"I'm a mess, Poppy. Seriously, I don't know what I'm doing. Right after the crawlspace incident, Lavender stopped by the house and told me how the B&B is under attack online." Poppy gave a confused look and Daisy filled her in on the details.

"Oh man, Daisy, I'm so sorry."

"I just want to get online and blast the liars!"

"I bet. What does Lavender say?" Poppy asked.

Daisy shared the game plan. Then she added, "If I just knew who it was, maybe I could stop it. Or at least retaliate."

"Well, I don't think 'eye for an eye' is a great strategy."

"I do hate that 'turn the other cheek' passage," Daisy frowned.

"Pray about it. Maybe God has something He is working out," Poppy offered.

"That's good advice." Daisy admitted. "Thanks."

"As for Lance..." Poppy studied her with brown eyes, "Same advice," Poppy finished. "Pray about it. Maybe the answer will surprise you."

13

"*H*onestly, no wonder your family calls you Daze. Could you have your head further up in the clouds?" Lance felt the irritation simmering.

Daisy held up her hands in front of her chest, as if in surrender. "Look, I'm sorry. How was I supposed to know the difference between sanded grout and unsanded grout?"

Considering they'd covered the same topic three weeks ago when they grouted the bathrooms upstairs, he expected her to remember. Lance stuffed down the sarcastic remark and dug his keys out of his pocket while jogging down the porch steps.

When Daisy opened the passenger door and

climbed inside, he gave a sideways glance. "What are you doing?"

"I'm coming with you."

"No, you're not," he said. Seriously? This entire trip was her fault and now she wanted to come?

"I am coming to the hardware store so you can show me what I did wrong when I picked grout for the kitchen." Daisy buckled her seatbelt and crossed her arms. "This is nonnegotiable."

In response, Lance turned the key and revved the engine. This woman was going to give him an aneurysm. They were all ready to grout the tile flooring in the kitchen, but just as Lance cut the top off the bag of grout, he saw it was the wrong kind. Things like this were why renovations should be left to detail-oriented people like him. If he had a dollar for every time he'd reminded Flower Power over there to 'measure twice and cut once', he'd be able to buy the bed-and-breakfast out from under her.

Their whole morning was derailed and instead of finishing the floor, they would waste most of the morning on a trip to the hardware store. Which meant sitting in the tiny cab of his truck with Daisy, when she could have stayed at the house and done something. Anything other than sit here and smell like the vanilla and honey he remembered from the crawlspace.

"I know you are perfect and you've never made a mistake in your life—"

Lance turned at the comment, studying her in the passenger seat. "You think I've never made a mistake?" She breathed heavily from the confrontation and he waited. Daisy was beautiful when she was angry. Her green eyes flashed with silver.

"You've never done anything spontaneous in your entire life, Lance Matthews." The set of her jaw challenged him and he curled his fists.

She wanted spontaneous? He leaned across the center console and reached behind her neck. Lance pulled Daisy to him, covering her lips with his. The intensity of their exchange simmered within the kisses, each unwilling to surrender and determined to prove their point. Lance pulled her closer, heat rising within him as he heard her sigh into the kiss, and he tasted her surrender.

Lance softened his kiss and treasured the last moments before it would end. They'd been down this road and decided it was a mistake. But somehow, she continued to get under his skin. Daisy was right, he didn't do spontaneous—kissing her aside. But she was wrong if she thought he'd never made mistakes. This was an exceptional example.

When they broke the kiss, Daisy's soft breath warmed his lips as he resisted the need to create space between them. Here, too close for words, was a good place. Words just got in the way. With a sigh, Lance pulled back and released her, retreating to the safety of his side of the truck.

Apparently, he had shocked the words out of her. They drove in silence to the hardware store, nearly twenty miles away in Minden. It was a smaller store, but closer than the others. Every minute spent in the truck with Daisy was torture. As much as he loved restoring the house, Lance would be glad when it was over. He'd tried making lists of all the reasons Daisy wasn't right for him. Long, long lists.

His heart clearly hadn't gotten the message, because Lance kept trying to talk himself into reasons it would work—the obvious being the smoldering kisses. Then things like this fiasco with the grout happened, and he remembered the entire list all over again.

Quickly, Lance placed two bags of sanded grout into the small shopping cart.

Daisy studied the bag. "I'm sorry I messed up earlier, Lance. Can you take a minute and talk me through it again?" Part of him was disappointed she didn't want to talk about the kiss. The rest of him was grateful.

Daisy's fire had dimmed, genuine interest replacing her defensive attitude from earlier. The glint of determination in her eyes mirrored ones he had seen before, like when she'd crossed the wires of an outlet.

Lance took a deep breath and walked through the label on the bag, comparing the options. Finally, he quizzed Daisy about hypothetical projects and the proper material.

"I would use... sanded." Daisy said, hesitating while she considered, but confident in her eventual answer.

A broad smile stretched across his face and Lance held up his hand for a high five. "Perfect. You've got it down." He started pushing the cart toward the front counter. "Now, let's get out of here and see if we can't get started on this."

"Sounds good. While we are in town, do you want to grab lunch at the bistro?"

It was a bit early for lunch, but the memory of the few times he'd eaten at B&J Bistro made his mouth water. Whoever was in the kitchen these days was a magician.

After Daisy paid for the grout, they tossed the bags in the back of his truck and walked down the block to B&J Bistro. Lance had spent time in Minden; it wasn't far from his hometown of Greencastle, and the annual Fall Festival was the best in the area. Which, he realized, he'd already missed this year.

How could tomorrow be Thanksgiving? Soon it would be Christmas and then, in January, he would turn thirty-five. Many of his friends were raising teenagers. Here he was, still single.

Lance had his friends, business, and church. But, as he watched Daisy embrace and start chatting with the manager at the bistro, he had to admit something was missing.

"Lance, have you met Chrissy? She owns this place; isn't it amazing?" Chrissy flushed at the compliment.

"Nice to meet you, ma'am. It really is incredible." Lance was impressed. He'd assumed she was just a staff member, but to realize she owned it? "I remember coming here with my dad when it was Bud and Janine's. I'm glad it's still around."

Chrissy nodded, "Me too. It's been a crazy year getting everything running and planning our wedding. But it's been a dream come true to turn this place into what it is today! Todd and I have a lot to be thankful for this year."

After directing them to a table and wishing them a Happy Thanksgiving, Chrissy bounced off to the kitchen, and a waitress came over to take their orders.

The frustration of the morning and the tension between them eased. They talked about the house and unfinished projects, but segued easily into conversations about family and hobbies and church.

Lance's anger rose when Daisy told him more about the online bashing. It was obvious that if Daisy could have jumped across the table and tackled the person trashing her business, she would have done so.

"Hold up there, Feisty Pants. It'll be alright. For one, as soon as actual people start leaving reviews, those negative stories will disappear into the shuffle. And the place is amazing. I will definitely recommend it to all of my friends looking for a weekend getaway."

She gave him a grateful smile and his pulse skyrocketed. "I know, I know. You're right, it just drives me crazy not to know who is doing this. More than anything, I want this bed-and-breakfast to succeed."

"Why did you choose to do a B&B, anyway?"

Lance was curious. The renovation part seemed to fit Daisy, despite her scatterbrained tendencies. But where did running a hotel fit in?

Her fork scraped the plate, scratching patterns in the remnants of her hollandaise sauce. "I love the idea of inviting people from all over into my home and making them feel welcome. Like my mom does. Have you met her yet?"

Lance shook his head in response and she continued, "My entire life, she has been caring for the kids of her friends, opening our house to relatives and visiting missionaries." Daisy glanced up at him, and Lance resisted the temptation to push a strand of hair from her eyes. "I can't wait to decorate it and make it homey. I have all kinds of ideas to make it special for my guests. It's been a dream for a while now. And I've let too many of my dreams die. So, I'm not letting this one go." When she shook her head, her hair shifted. Lance saw the passion had overwhelmed her, and tears brimmed in Daisy's eyes.

Admiration filled Lance; an unseen side of Daisy was sitting across from him. Daisy didn't just want to make old things new by doing the renovation. She wanted to use that to bless others and show hospitality. Daisy had always been kind and thoughtful. Maybe he had just been caught up their differences and had overlooked the good things about her creative and adaptable nature.

Being flexible would be a key skill in running a hotel. Last minute reservations or cancelations, impromptu requests or problems? None of it could be planned for. Which would absolutely drive him insane, like the plan for this morning being derailed by a simple mistake.

But Daisy the Dreamer? She would thrive in that environment and make her guests feel right at home. Wanting to affirm her dream and convey his confidence in her ability, Lance laid his hand on the table, outstretched toward her.

Daisy stared at it, her gaze traveling up his arm when he spoke. "Bloom's Farm Bed and Breakfast is going to be everything you've imagined it to be. I believe in you, Daisy Bloom. God has uniquely gifted you to pursue this dream." Then, to lighten the mood, he added, "Even if those particular aspects of your personality sometimes make me crazy."

Daisy sniffled a laugh and wiped the dampness from her eyes with her napkin. She placed her hand in his for a moment, her touch a jolt to his system like a shot of espresso. "Thanks. I needed to hear that." She squeezed his hand before pulling back. "Sometimes it is easy to forget God has everything in his hand and I need to give control to Him."

Her words struck Lance, echoing and wriggling their way deep into his thoughts. She needed to give control to Him. Had Lance done that? Or was he still trying to control things according to his endless lists, plans, and schedules?

14

*D*aisy's back ached from the constant bending and scraping and washing of the grouting process. She sat at her tiny bistro table on Thursday morning, now positioned just outside the kitchen, waiting for the grout to set. She and Lance hadn't finished until after seven the night before.

Hawthorne tramped down the stairs and appeared through the side entrance of the dining room, freshly showered. Impromptu caution tape— blue painters tape— blocked both entrances to the kitchen, forming a giant crisscross pattern across the openings.

"Didn't I hear you get up super early this morning?" she asked, vaguely remembering the sound of footsteps on the stairs.

Hawthorne grinned and grabbed the seat across from her. "I helped Rose with the animals. But Avery should get here any minute." Her brother's joy was contagious and Daisy couldn't help but smile back.

"I'm glad she gets to hang out here for Thanksgiving. It must be hard for her not to see her family, though."

"That's why she's coming over so early. I think we're taking the horses out."

Daisy gave him a skeptical look. "Isn't it like forty degrees outside?"

Hawthorne wiggled his eyebrows and responded, "Maybe we'll just have to share a horse to stay warm, then."

Daisy threw an empty soda can at him, laughing when the last few drops sprinkled his jacket."

"Gross, Daze!" he said while brushing the beads of soda with his hands. Noise outside the window grabbed his attention and they both looked to see Avery's car pull into the gravel driveway.

"Have fun with Avery. I'll see you up at the main house," Hawthorne was already out the room and nearly to the front door so she yelled after him, "for board games and lunch!"

Daisy tried not the feel envious when her brother and her friend embraced after Hawthorne helped Avery from the car. She'd always been fine being single. Even turning thirty last year hadn't been a big deal.

But if Hawthorne and Avery were getting serious, would he move out? Most of her siblings had dated throughout the years. Well, except Lily. But Lily didn't share much. There was more to that story Daisy didn't know. But none of her siblings had serious relationships before.

Hawthorne and Avery seemed to be gettings serious though. She and Hawthorne had been seeing each other a lot. Daisy even heard her brother's low voice talking with Avery late into the night.

Daisy pulled out her phone and read the verse of the day from her Bible app. She had much to be thankful for. Her family, her friends, and her house. Even if a house couldn't talk back or take you on a romantic horseback ride.

It wasn't quite as cold as Daisy expected, the bright sun chasing away the chill on her walk. She would be early, but no doubt her mom needed help.

They always played board games and watched the parade and football during the day, too.

With her mom's instruction, Daisy mixed casseroles from recipes on wrinkled notecards, and opened cans of yams, chatting with her mom and sisters. Rose wasn't there and neither was her dad, but she knew they would come back from the barn soon to snack on appetizers while everyone waited impatiently for the turkey.

The front door burst open, and Daisy heard her name being yelled. Was that Avery?

When Avery came around the corner, out of breath and pale, the chatter in the kitchen died and Daisy's heart raced. "What's wrong, Aves?"

Between gasps of air, Avery spoke quickly. "Your dad had a stroke. Down at the animal barn. The ambulance is on the way." Her mom scurried around the island and out the front door. Daisy stood unmoving as her sisters started asking questions.

"Is he okay?"

"Where's Hawthorne?"

"Let's go," Daisy finally said, grabbing a hand towel and wiping off the milk she'd splashed.

Daisy and Poppy had started making their way to the front door when Lavender spoke up, "Let's grab mom's car. She's probably freezing and halfway to the barn by now."

On their way back through the kitchen, Daisy spotted Lily trying to turn off the stove and restore the kitchen to order, while Avery shooed her away. Gratitude for her friend filled her as they filed into the garage and the oversized SUV. They needed to get to Dad as soon as possible.

LANCE DODGED A TODDLER, barely avoiding the red sticky fingers aimed directly at his khakis. Who thought giving a two-year-old their own piece of cherry pie was a good idea? It sounded like something Daisy would do.

Thanksgiving for the Matthews had always been at his grandmother's house until she passed away. Since then, his dad's family had congregated at his Aunt Diane's house. His cousins were like siblings to him, and he was like an uncle to their kids.

The almost unpleasant feeling in his gut directly resulted from the two full plates he'd eaten, followed by the enormous slice of pumpkin pie he'd devoured with intentional disregard for the protest of his full stomach. There was nothing quite like Thanksgiving with family.

His dad laid claim to the recliner and was reading books with Lance's cousin's twin boys. Seeing the identical faces, a swipe of whipped cream still gracing the cheek of one, brought his thoughts circling around, yet again, to Daisy. She must miss her twin today.

Before he had a chance to over-analyze his actions, Lance pulled out his cellphone and tapped out a quick holiday greeting to the woman who was never far from his thoughts. They'd worked past dark yesterday finishing the grout, using bright, portable work lights to compensate for the lack of daylight.

Lance tucked his phone away and laid on the floor, groaning in relief at the space it created in his gluttonous stomach and the stretch in his back, which ached from the time spent bent over grouting.

He might have fallen asleep, he couldn't be sure. A high-pitched exclamation startled Lance into awareness.

"Dog pile!" He recognized the phrase a split-second before the tumbling body of a five-year-old came into view mid-air above him. The instinctive flinch and tuck wasn't quite fast enough and the sudden impact rocked his entire body, forcing out a grunt. Smaller impacts registered and the five-year-old squealed as his cousins joined the dog pile.

"Oh no! You woke up the dragon!" Lance yelled. He lifted his arms and made claws with his hands as the kids squealed with laughter. He roared and sat up, small bodies surrounding him as he pretended to trap them and chased them around the small living room as the other adults looked on.

Once Lance was completely and totally worn out, he extricated himself from the barrage of tiny humans and escaped to the kitchen. The food still on the counters tempted him, despite the feast he'd consumed only an hour ago. The intermittent vibration of his phone in his pocket had been pulling his thoughts away from his wrestling partners throughout play time. Lance pulled it out and saw a handful of messages from the last hour.

He read them quickly, and his lighthearted spirit fell.

Dad had a stroke. At the hospital.

Worst Thanksgiving ever.

I hope you are having a good time with your family.

I'm a basket case.

Can you talk?

The time stamp on the last message was only five minutes ago, and Lance hit the call button.

The whisper of Daisy's voice reached out to him through the phone, "Hey."

They'd never really talked on the phone before, and Lance didn't know what to say, but he asked, "How's your dad?"

A sniffle meant Daisy was crying and Lance felt his heart break a little more. "We don't know. The doctor said we have to wait and see—" Daisy's voice broke at the end.

"I'm so sorry, Daisy. What do you need?"

She laughed through her tears, "I don't even know. I'm just a wreck. How could this happen? My dad's in the best shape of anyone I know!"

"Do you want me to come there?" Lance didn't even know why he offered. They barely got along most of the time, why would she want him to come? Still, she'd texted him and asked him to talk. Maybe she needed him. If she did, he would be there in an instant.

"No, don't come. I need to be with my sisters. Stay with your family. I just needed..." Her thoughts trailed off and Lance heard her sigh. This was a deeper expression of exhaustion than she'd made in the months they'd been working together. "I don't know. I'm sorry I interrupted your day," she said apologetically, putting an end to whatever train of thought she had started.

"Don't worry about it, Daisy. I'm here if you change your mind." She thanked him absently before hanging up. How awful for the entire Bloom family to have this happen, especially on a day expected to be full of joy and thankfulness. They needed to stay together. But part of him wished she would change her mind and ask him to be there, too.

Which was crazy, because most of the time Lance thought about how ready he was to get away from Daisy. But hearing the pain in her voice on the phone made him want to wrap her in his arms and carry that burden for her. Daisy was too proud to let him, and they both agreed there was no future. Blurring the lines of friendship and coworkers would be a bad idea.

While Lance stared at the black screen of his phone, his father's voice startled him. "What's wrong, son?" Greg hobbled into the kitchen, using the cane required by his physical therapist.

Lance glanced up and told his dad about Keith Bloom's stroke.

"Poor girl must be worried sick," his dad said. Lance pressed his lips together and nodded his head absently. What could he do? "Would you like us to pray for them?" The offer came effortlessly from his father, his first instinct in the face of trouble, and Lance nodded gratefully.

His dad laid a hand on Lance's shoulder and leaned in to pray quietly, a conversation only Lance, Greg, and God would hear. It settled Lance's troubled heart and he gave his dad a quick hug when they finished. He pulled up Daisy's contact info and sent a message.

I am praying. Here if you need me. It didn't seem like enough, but Lance knew prayers were not just a last resort, but a front-line weapon. A weapon for healing and to ward off worry, exhaustion, and anger seemed like exactly what the Bloom family needed today.

15

*J*ust this morning, Daisy thought how different her brother was and how responsible he'd been. What a load of baloney! This afternoon at the hospital, Hawthorne took off and was nowhere to be found. Poppy just talked to Avery and she hadn't seen him either. Wanting to see his fiancée after the incident made sense, but he hadn't done that.

Truth was, Daisy would rather be almost anywhere than the depressing waiting room of the hospital. But her obligation to her family was too strong to leave. She'd nearly agreed when Lance offered to come, and Daisy wasn't even in a relationship with him! But Hawthorne bailed on the entire family without a word. Their mom assumed he went back to the farm to help Rose with the animals, but Rose already called to say he wasn't there.

It had been the longest day of her life, and Daisy wanted nothing more than to collapse into her bed. Okay, maybe that wasn't true. She also wanted a hug from someone big and strong who could squeeze some warmth back into the day. Which is why she needed Hawthorne—other than her dad, who was currently lying in a hospital bed, Hawthorne was the only man in her life she should be hugging.

Thoughts of Lance intruded on her exhaustion. Were they at that level? Being held by Lance would be dangerous. She wasn't even sure you could call them friends, although the last few weeks had been a confusing mixture of friendship and... more. He'd kissed her twice now, and she'd kissed him back. But hugging? It seemed more intimate.

Daisy was proud of her independent woman status, and she'd been pushing back the desire to lean on someone else all day. It was still there, though. Did every woman have that desire? Even the strongest women she saw conquering companies and impacting politics? Did they get lonely or want to collapse on the shoulder of a big, strong man? Daisy was the pathetic princess from a children's movie, incapable of rescuing herself and waiting for the handsome prince to save the day. She didn't want to need anyone.

Daisy opened the door to the old house and walked upstairs on autopilot, straight past the other rooms and into her bedroom. She spotted a note on the bed in Lance's distinctive neat, block letters.

If you are up for it, I left a gift in the north bathroom. Rest up.

Her brow wrinkled and Daisy backtracked, walking into the north bedroom and the attached bath. On the counter sat a fluffy white towel, a lighter, two candles, and a bottle of body wash with a loofah. She studied the candles and the soap, all labeled "Stress Relief". There was a bottle of painkillers, with a post-it. *If your back felt like mine this morning, you need these. I fixed the rain shower, too.*

That stupid rain shower had been giving them problems since the beginning, and they finally sent it back to the manufacturer for a replacement.

Lance came over and did this for her today? The giant-pile-of-ooze feeling was back, and Daisy started to cry again. With blurry vision, she lit the candles. Maybe not needing anyone was overrated. Daisy let the water run hot and finally stepped into the spray, letting it wash away her tears. After only a moment,

Daisy sank to the floor of the shower like any good pile of ooze should. Then, she pulled her knees to her chest.

She sobbed loudly, letting the warm water run down her face and drown out the sound. The floor and walls of the tile shower were cold and hard, a stark contrast to the warmth falling on top of her in a steady beat.

Here, finally alone in her house, it was safe to break down. Even in the hospital surrounded by her sisters, Daisy hadn't wanted to really let it out. There was something about sitting in the shower that made it okay. No one would find her or judge her.

Her dad, the man she'd always looked up to, had nearly died today. She'd avoided even thinking those words until now, too afraid that she might think them into existence. Instead, Daisy had taken her fear and her worry and her panic, and she'd stuffed it deep inside, focusing on the next minute. And the next.

Move to another chair.

Pace the room.

Watch the nurses.

Hug her sisters.

Until finally, the day was over.

Daisy had been emotionally broken before—lying in her own hospital bed, her leg in a cast. The timing with her new dance partner had been barely off, her balance shifted only slightly.

Those seemingly minuscule deviations were the difference between a flawless landing and a broken ankle. Between her debut performance with the professional dance company and the end of a career that never really started.

According to the doctor, differences in millimeters in the blood clot could mean the distinction between brain dead and perfectly functional. Between losing his movement or losing his speech. Her father was the voice of the family. He prayed over them. He cheered them on from the sidelines, with his loud yells and embarrassing commentary. Would that ever happen again? Would Keith Bloom get to watch his grandkids play soccer or star in their first dance recital? What would he miss?

A fresh wave of grief washed over her. It wasn't fair! Why would God do this? Her parents had the strongest faith of anyone she knew. Bitterness crept in, casting shadows of doubt on the prayers she and her sisters had offered today in the waiting room. Had they been empty words of faith? Or did she truly believe God was in control?

Unable to answer her own questions, she watched the water cascade over her knees and swirl down the drain, unable to focus on anything beyond the tiny tiled cave in which she hid. If she never left this shower, could she avoid her new reality?

The water stayed warm as she sat for endless minutes. Maybe hours. Until the tears finally subsided and she picked herself up off the hard shower floor. Moving slowly, each limb impossibly heavy, Daisy finished her shower before turning off the water and wrapping herself in the luxurious white towel Lance swiped from the boxes of hotel supplies downstairs.

Good to know her guests would enjoy good towels anyway, regardless of what the online reviews claimed. Plus, an excellent shower. She had a new appreciation for the tankless water heater Lance had installed. They were random, misfit thoughts that sprung up in the pool of defeated worries of the day. If her thoughts had been arranged on a page, she could circle "one of these things is not like the others" in vivid red ink. Lance was a bright spot in the cloudy haze of the hardest day of her life.

Unwilling to analyze that particular thought further, Daisy blew out the candles and shuffled back to her own room. It seemed like too much effort to even pick up her feet. She poked her head into

Hawthorne's room—just in case—and the last ray of hope about him disappeared.

Whatever. Maybe Avery could sort him out. For now, Daisy wouldn't do anything except collapse into bed and let the day be blessedly over. No doubt tomorrow wouldn't be easy, but it couldn't possibly be harder than today.

16

*L*ance texted Daisy over the weekend, but it was finally Monday and he had an excuse to come see her in person. He needed to see for himself that she was okay.

Daisy did text him Friday morning and had seemed grateful for the surprise he'd left. The candles and soap were his Aunt Diane's idea, and she sent him with the gift set she'd been 'saving for the right person'. Still, it was so hard to read emotion in text messages.

Lance pulled up to the house just after seven on Monday morning, eager to see her face for himself. The vibe between them had been confusing since the beginning. Crawlspace kisses. Flirty banter and deep conversation. Truck cab kisses and an unspoken agreement to ignore them entirely. Then Thanksgiving. Had he crossed a line by inserting himself into that miserable day?

The house was quiet when Lance tapped on the door, but he let himself inside and looked around. It felt like everything had changed over the weekend, yet the house looked the same. Sure, there were a few more empty Diet Dr. Pepper cans in the kitchen, and microwave dinner boxes filled the trashcan, but other than that? Everything, physically at least, was the same as when he'd left Wednesday night.

Lance gathered empty soda cans and tossed them in the trash, then he removed the bag to take it outside. A sleepy yawn sounded behind him and he turned. Clad in leggings and an oversized sweater, a drowsy and confused Daisy stretched as she walked into the kitchen. "What time is it?" she asked through another yawn.

Lance finished pulling the trash out and shook out a new bag. "Almost 7:30," he said, stretching the truth a little, since it was actually only about ten after.

Daisy murmured her surprise and sat at the bistro table, still in the dining room. Streamers of blue painter's tape hung limply from the door frame where they had been torn through but not removed.

"How are you doing?" he asked softly, sitting across from her. The trash bag remained next to the bin, an unfinished job begging for his attention, but Lance needed to talk to Daisy; everything else would have to wait. There was nothing more important than being here for her.

"I'm fine," she said, but her attempt to smile was anything but reassuring. Daisy stared at a spot on the wall, clearly not processing at full speed.

Lance stepped over to the fridge and pulled out a Diet Dr. Pepper and set it in front of Daisy. She gave him a half-smile, but didn't move to open it. His concern deepened; that was not a good sign.

He reached over and popped the top of the soda, pushing it closer to Daisy. Please drink it. For some reason, it seemed critically important she do the blessedly normal action of drinking her beloved Diet Dr. Pepper. It was a small thing—but it seemed a monumental sign that she would be okay.

Daisy didn't reach over for it, though. She glanced up at him, her grayish-green eyes meeting Lance's for a moment before moving past him to a spot in the next room, cutting through his defenses with her own guardedness. "He's supposed to slay the giants," she said blankly, not allowing any emotion into her words.

At least she was talking, even if it was in cryptic, jumbled thoughts.

"Your dad?" he asked.

Daisy nodded slowly, her gaze sliding back to his. "What will I do without him?" A glimpse of the vulnerable and worried daughter peeked through the walls she'd constructed.

Lance didn't know what to say. Daisy was terrified of losing her father, and his dad dying had never crossed his mind. He had no solution for her pain and it was breaking him. "What do the doctors say?" he asked, carefully watching her face.

Daisy pressed her fingers to her eyes and rubbed her face with a moan. "They don't know. He still can't talk and he is weak. I've never seen him so..." Lance waited for her to find the word, "defeated." She shook her head and hugged her leg. "They say he'll continue to recover over the next weeks and months. But they can't say how much he'll ever be able to do. We just don't know." Daisy's voice broke on the last sentence and she laid her forehead on her knee.

Lance didn't know Keith well but he couldn't help but like the vivacious, bold personality of the Bloom family patriarch. "I'm so sorry, Daisy. What can I do?"

He wanted to hold her but wasn't sure if he could. The urge to step around the table and pull Daisy up and into his arms was overwhelming. But there was too much undefined between them. Wasn't there?

She sniffled and shook her head. "I don't know." Her other foot came up on the chair and she hugged both knees tighter, as though holding herself together while curled in a ball on the tiny bistro chair.

Screw it. "Come here." Lance touched her hand and tugged gently, pulling her toward him after she lowered her feet to the floor. He pulled her onto his lap, tucking her head onto his shoulder and stroking her hair. "Shhh. It's okay, sweetheart." Daisy relaxed into his embrace and wept quietly while he held her. She was so strong. And because he knew her strength, Lance knew what it cost her to break down. Her vulnerability was strength in itself, and unspeakably beautiful to him.

Lance felt the nudge to pray, and ignoring his self-consciousness, he whispered a prayer over her with his chin resting on the crown of her head. He prayed for comfort and strength for her and for miraculous healing for her father. When he finished, Lance shifted gently and kissed her hair. Maybe he was crossing the line, but it felt so right. Seeing Daisy hurting called to every protective and compassionate fiber of his being.

He was tired of fighting the feelings, trying to convince himself that she wasn't right for him. Lance couldn't argue with the rightness of this feeling. Daisy needed him right now. And for once, he wasn't going to fight it.

Daisy's lips twitched as Lance teased the top ruffle on the curtains he was hanging. He leaned back, trying to gain perspective and reached in again to adjust a spot, moving it until it was fluffed to his satisfaction.

Hiding her lips behind her soda can, Daisy smiled at his attention to detail. It was amusing to see the capable contractor laser-focused on ruffled window treatments. Lance turned to her and asked, "Does it look okay?"

Daisy nodded with pressed lips, and Lance wrinkled his brow, "Do they?"

The laugh she'd been restraining slipped out, and she grabbed his hand, pulling him down from the step ladder. "Yes! They look amazing. Thank you." Her arms slid around his waist and she tipped her head up for a kiss. "You are amazing."

He gave her a skeptical look but kissed her again. "I'll get back up and fix them if you want me too!"

In response, Daisy just shook her head and tightened her hold on him. "They look great. Seriously." They'd been taking it slow, easing their way into projects and tackling smaller things in between Daisy's visits to the hospital and the main house or the barn to help Rose.

Daisy had been embarrassed to break down in the kitchen with Lance, but after the hot tears had subsided, only the warmth of Lance's embrace remained. It had been really nice. Unsurprisingly, perhaps, given their previous fireworks in the crawl-space. But this was different; it wasn't fireworks. It was the gentle glow of a candle, spreading much needed light into the abject darkness of her days since Thanksgiving.

Instead of fighting his affection, she leaned into it— celebrating something positive in the emotionally draining marathon of hospital visits, worry, and farm obligations. Which might be why she was viewing Lance's perfectionist obsession with the proper amount of 'ruffle' on the curtains with amusement instead of impatience. It was kind of adorable how he wanted it to be just right and kept looking for her affirmation that it was satisfactory. As though she cared that much.

Lance nodded, "Okay. If you say so." Finally, he returned her hug and put his arms around her.

"I do," she said, looking up at him. "What should we do now?"

"I've got a few ideas," he murmured before his lips met hers. Daisy let the kiss carry her away, and she could have sworn her feet left the ground and the world spun around them. They were lost in time and space in a world all their own. The constant weight of her collective anxieties—about her father, the bed-and-breakfast, and even Andi in the Middle East—lightened. When they broke the kiss, she tucked her head into his shoulder and sighed. It was just a momentary reprieve from the cycle of worried thoughts she knew would return, but it was enough.

Lance gave her one last squeeze and loosened his arms, stepping away and creating space between them. Unwanted space, but probably needed, if she was honest. It would be easy to move too quickly. She may have known Lance for a few months, but this intimacy—emotional and physical—was new.

It was exciting but a little scary too. Daisy hadn't been in a relationship in years. Was this a relationship? It felt like one. They'd texted all weekend and she'd broken down in his arms yesterday. This morning they were kissing and working and then kissing again. It was almost like before, except that the bickering had been replaced with flirting.

It was a welcome replacement. Fighting with Lance was exhausting. Partly because he was mostly right, which was terribly difficult for her to admit and she would never do it to his face. And partly because he was just so intense. It was a waste of energy to verbally spar with him on every point she would prefer to. That had been the case from day one.

Lance probably felt like she fought him every step of the way, but she actually let a lot of things go without comment, unless she felt like getting under his skin. It had always been a bit of a source of enter-tainment to push his buttons and watch the fire in his eyes. The secret was not going too far. Sometimes, she didn't know his limit until after he had reached it.

Oh well. It had kept things interesting this far.

17

*L*ater in the week, Daisy and Lance were installing trim in the kitchen and dining room. A portly man in a starched dress shirt and shiny hard hat with the county logo, strode into the house without knocking. Daisy fought back a groan—the county inspector.

"Miss Bloom, I presume?" He extended his hand. After she shook it, he pulled out a small bottle of hand sanitizer and applied it to his surprisingly soft hands. She glanced at Lance and gave him an are-you-seeing-this look. His bemused expression made her smile despite her irritation at the impromptu visitor.

"How may I help you?"

"I'm Larry Havershem, the new county building

inspector. There have been a few complaints made to the planning and zoning commission about your project here. Namely—"

Daisy pounded her fist on the banister in frustration. "Are you kidding me?"

The man continued as if she hadn't spoken. "—concerns that the property does not meet required building and electrical codes and would not be safe for habitation, let alone for the planned operation as temporary lodging, that is to say—a hotel or motel."

The nasally tone of his voice made Daisy want to toss him out the window. Through clenched teeth, she growled, "It's a bed-and-breakfast."

"Yes, well, we will see about that, won't we?" Daisy's mouth dropped open and she was about to let Havershem have a piece of her mind when Lance came up beside her. With one solid hand on her shoulder, her anger dimmed.

Lance stuck out his hand. "Lance Matthews, I'm the contractor on this project. Can I help you with something specific?"

The man introduced himself and handed Lance a document. Daisy stepped next to Lance and grabbed the papers, holding them so she could read while Lance looked over her shoulder. Skimming the page revealed a long list of bogus complaints. Unsafe drinking water. Electrical fire hazards. Animal infestation. Structural deficiencies.

Lance gave a low whistle. "That's quite a long list. I am more than happy to show you that each of these complaints is unfounded, Mr. Havershem. Where would you like to begin? The crawl space, perhaps?" Daisy almost choked at the comment, even though it had been delivered with no hint of sarcasm or malice. Oh, Lance was good.

The inspector's eyes bulged, and he backtracked. "No that won't be necessary today. Perhaps you can show me the," he checked the list, "circuit breaker? And the, uh, water quality tests?"

Lance smiled. "Absolutely." He led the inspector down the hallway and into the small utility room. All the wiring had been replaced, with Greg's help, and the inspector made notes on his page. He didn't look happy about it though.

"The water quality?" he asked in the pinched, condescending voice that made Daisy snarl.

"You want to know about the water quality?" She grabbed a plastic cup from the table and filled it from the kitchen sink. She drank deeply. She grabbed another cup and filled it up, then shoved it into the inspector's hands. "Drink it."

Havershem held the cup far away from himself

as though she had handed him a container filled with worms. "I will not!"

Frustration bubbled over and Daisy yelled at him, "Drink it!"

"Ma'am, there have been complaints filed about the quality of the water here and the county—"

"Oh, baloney! I demand to know where these complaints are coming from!" Lance laid a hand on her shoulder, but she didn't stop. "They are wasting your time! This is all a part of this ridiculous smear campaign. Someone is trying to destroy my business and I will not stand for it!"

"Mr. Havershem, maybe today isn't the best time. It's been a bit of a difficult week for the family and—"

Daisy's eyes grew wide and she pointed a finger at Lance. "This is not about my father."

"I know, I know." Lance pulled her into his arms and spoke over her shoulder. "We will be happy to pull the records for water quality tests on the well water, or perform some if they haven't been done recently."

"We will need tests completed in the last six months," the inspector replied curtly.

While Lance ushered him out, Daisy wandered back through the dining room, muttering to herself and wiping the tears she was furious at herself for crying. Wasn't there a limit on how many tears a girl could cry in a week?

Daisy was still struggling to figure out what normal looked like. Her dad was still in the hospital, and Mom was spending every day there with him. The rest of the family had settled on rotating morning and afternoons to sit with their parents. Daisy was scheduled for this afternoon.

Thankfully, Hawthorne actually came through. He'd shown up in the middle of the night and called a family meeting for Friday morning, during which they divvied up roles and responsibilities.

None of which really impacted Daisy, except to step in as needed when her sisters asked for help. Lily was staying at the house and playing mama bear —stocking the refrigerator with healthy snacks and making sure their mother didn't completely fall apart.

They were all trying to make sure their mother wouldn't fall apart. Which would be hard for Daisy since she couldn't keep herself from doing so. The inspector stopping by with these complaints seemed like a cruel joke. Could she handle more?

The buzz of her phone's text message notification went off in her pocket. The message from Lavender answered her question.

New reviews popping up over the weekend. Stay the course, sis.

If there was a limit on tears, Daisy apparently hadn't reached it yet.

SOMETIMES, a girl needed her mom. But Laura Bloom was entrenched in a crisis of her own, giving every iota of energy to Keith. When Daisy went to the hospital in the afternoon, she planned to tell her mom about the reviews and the inspector. But watching her mom rubbing her dad's hand tenderly and reading to him from the Bible or the newspaper, Daisy knew she couldn't add to her mother's burden.

Instead, she walked down to the hospital atrium and called the next best thing to a mother—her godmother, a family friend affectionately called Aunt Jacquie. Jacquie Dowdy had been part of the family for as long as her parents had been married. Daisy's parents had figured as they had more children, each would need someone they had a special connection with who they didn't have to share with siblings. Jacquie was that person for Daisy.

Her godmother had worked her way up the corporate ladder until retiring from her final position as CEO of a multi-million-dollar company. Through the years, Daisy and Jacquie had talked and gone on trips. Plus, Jacquie loved the Lord with all her heart and would be the perfect person to help sort things out.

The call was short, but Jacquie invited her over for dinner. Daisy went back upstairs to kiss her tired parents goodbye.

"I love you both," she said.

At Jacquie's house, she was greeted with a warm, soft hug and instantly wrapped in her godmother's expensive perfume. Jacquie's ever-present silver jewelry chimed gently as she ushered Daisy in. "Oh, child. It's so good to see you! How are things at the house?" When Daisy first considered renovating the old house, she'd asked for Jacquie's opinion before presenting the idea to her parents.

Daisy talked about the renovations and invited Jacquie out for a tour. "Plus, I'm saving a room for you and Roger to stay on opening weekend."

"Wonderful!" Jacquie clapped her hands together and sat them in her lap. "On the phone, you said you needed to talk about something specific. Whatever it is, I'll do my best to help."

The words had been building up and rolling around in her mind for several days, and at the invitation, she released the entire story along with all her feelings and fears. Daisy cried and talked about how her father's stroke had shaken their whole family. She told Jacquie about the mystery person trying to sabotage the building, and how the inspector showed up and was causing headaches.

"I heard about your father through the church prayer chain, sweetie. I'm so sorry you are going through this. And the timing of everything else on top of it? I'm sure it's hard." Jacquie pulled her small, leather-bound Bible from the end table, as though just touching it would help her channel the right words.

"There was a time in my career when it seemed everyone was against me. I felt completely alone. I knew I was doing the right thing and that God had trusted me with something important. But there were people who didn't like what I was doing. They trashed me in the press and even brought lawsuits against me."

Disbelief and confusion filled Daisy, and she racked her brain for any memory of it happening, but couldn't. She gave a puzzled look to the motherly figure across from her.

"I think it was while you were in New York. Either way, I imagine that's a bit like you feel right now."

Daisy nodded, "That's exactly how I feel. What did you do, and what happened?"

"It was the longest year and a half of my life. But you know what?" Jacquie smiled and patted her Bible, "God saw me through it. He will do the same for you. Do what you know is the right thing—the godly thing—and remember that at the end of the day you only have to answer to God and yourself." Jacquie laughed softly, "I know you'll be tempted to lash back. I know I was! My reputation was important to me and people were dragging me through the mud. But my desire to fight back wasn't as important as the responsibility I was given, and not as important as my relationship with God."

"I can't believe I never heard this story." Daisy shook her head. It was encouraging to hear from someone who had walked through something similar.

Jacquie smiled, "Maybe God intended for you to hear it today."

"I think you might be right. I'm so grateful for you, Jacquie. Thanks so much for finding time for me today."

"Oh, pfft. I always have time for my goddaughter. Besides," Jacquie said with a twinkle in her eye, "I'm retired now, which means I get to fill my days with grandkids, books, and more time for the things I love."

Daisy asked for an update on Jacquie's grandkids, and the conversation shifted to more lighthearted topics. Daisy stayed for dinner with Jacquie and her husband, Roger. It was exactly the respite she needed from the farm and the constant barrage of fears, doubts, and to-do lists.

18

A familiar rhythm of knocks sounded at the door, and Lance glanced at Daisy.

"Hello? Miss Bloom?" The wheezy inspector's voice called through the house.

Lance caught Daisy's panicked look and mouthed, "Go!" while waving her toward the back door. This was the fourth time in a week Mr. Havershem had dropped by. It was getting ridiculous.

Lance was doing everything he could to help Daisy, including dealing with the inspector, who was turning out to be an even bigger turkey than it originally seemed. The man was getting on Lance's nerve, and he was typically a pretty patient guy, especially when dealing with the authorities.

Daisy was safely out of sight when the inspector

poked his head around the corner, clipboard in hand and pressed khakis making Lance roll his eyes. "Oh, hello, Mr. Havershem. How can I help you today?"

"I'm looking for Miss Bloom, is she here?"

Lance spoke as honestly as he could, trying not to laugh. "I'm sorry, you just missed her. There is a lot going on with the family right now, perhaps I could answer any questions you have?"

The inspector frowned and pulled a pen from his front pocket. "Hmm, that's unfortunate. I was hoping to review some of these complaints with her. Perhaps you can help." The inspector ran through a laundry-list of complaints, some were so far-fetched that Lance had to ask for clarification.

"Someone complained the roof had no support structure?"

"That is correct," Mr. Havershem said smugly.

Lance spoke slowly, "Well, I'm pretty certain if that were true, it would come crashing down on us. You know, since there would be nothing holding it up."

"I'm going to need to see it."

Irritation rising, Lance took the man to the attic access from the upstairs hallway. Maybe he would get bit by a spider while he was up there.

Finally, when the man had wasted about two

hours of Lance's time, he was finally ready to leave.

"You be sure to tell Miss Bloom I was here and I will be back to address any further complaints."

Minutes after the inspector left, Daisy peered around the corner from the back entry. "Is the coast clear?" she said with a stage whisper.

Lance felt the irritation evaporate at the sight of her. He nodded, and she jogged toward him. "Thank you. I don't think I could have dealt with him today." She raised to her tiptoes to kiss him.

"It's fine. I just wish we knew why he is so bent on shutting this down." He pulled Daisy into his arms and gave her a squeeze. "What do you say we get away for a bit? I think our momentum is shot, and I could go for something fun."

Daisy smiled. "That sounds great. I could use a distraction. Things with Dad are still progressing, but slowly. And Andi gets here next week. We could go pick up supplies for signs for the airport!" Daisy said excitedly.

It wasn't exactly what Lance had in mind, but it was better than nothing. They could hit the store for poster board and grab lunch. Maybe a movie? Cuddling up with Daisy in a dark theater sounded like a good way to kill a few hours.

It had been two weeks since Thanksgiving, and

every day, Lance was enjoying his new relationship with Daisy more and more. He hadn't been in a relationship for years. Too many women only saw him as a successful business owner, or their own personal handyman. And most of them came on too strong, trying to win him over from the first meeting.

Not Daisy, he thought with a smile. Their first meeting—their first month, in fact—had been something completely different, filled with verbal showdowns and sarcastic comments. Daisy was so independent, he knew she wasn't using him. And he was drawn to her unlike any woman he'd ever met. Every opportunity to touch her or hold her, Lance found himself initiating. When she came up behind him and laid her cheek between his shoulders, he felt like he could scale mountains.

And kissing Daisy? He leaned down and did just that. With her lips under his, his head was spinning and dipping like Daisy when she danced. She hadn't had much occasion for dancing lately; he recognized the stress in her shoulders and her eyes. Even laughing or flirting with him, there was a heaviness there he couldn't make go away.

"Let's go, then." Maybe focusing on Andi coming home would help Daisy release some of the worry. If that didn't help, maybe cuddling in the dark movie theater was just what she needed, too.

"I'M SORRY, Mr. Matthews, if you cannot find your permits and have them correctly displayed as required by County Code 3.2 subsection 11, I'm going to have to force you to halt all ongoing work."

The inspector was back again. Lance had the water quality tests done and gave them to the man. But, for the life of him, Lance could not find any paperwork showing that Daisy had pulled permits. His dad reassured him they had done everything to book, but when he asked Daisy, it only took two seconds of panicked look on her face to confirm she had no idea where the papers were.

Daisy leaped to her feet from her position on the stairs and yelled out, "You can't do that!"

The droning, whiny man continued his mono-logue, "In addition, Mr. Matthews, since you portend to be the contractor on this renovation, I will need to place all of your existing projects within the county jurisdiction on hold until further notice."

His stomach flipped, and Lance clenched his

fists. Was this a joke? "You have got to be kidding me!"

"I assure you, Mr. Matthews, I never 'kid' about matters of safety. I will check periodically to make sure no additional work has been performed."

"When I find my permit—which I will—what do we need to do?" Daisy asked, the pale, worried look on her face revealing the false confidence of her strong words.

"If you find your permit, Miss Bloom, you may reach out to my office and schedule an appointment. I will come out at my earliest convenience." Then he added with a smirk, "Typical wait time is one to two weeks after your call."

Lance hadn't been tempted to punch someone since junior high, but the man was dangerously close to pushing him over the edge. Not only was this property on hold, but his other jobs as well? Just great. This was a nightmare, and it was all because Space Cadet over there couldn't manage to keep her paperwork straight.

Lance pushed past the inspector and out of the house, leaving Daisy to deal with the mess she'd made. Despite his anger at the situation, he hated to leave Daisy like this. But, he had to go call Cody and

Jason to let them know to stop work if the permit was issued by the county. Daisy's haphazard approach to life was going to hurt his business.

He knew this was rotten luck and that Daisy hadn't done anything to deserve the interference or the online reviews trashing her business. But was it really so hard to stay organized and think things through?

It wasn't like it was any easier for him, but he'd trained himself over the years to keep track of things, finish what he started, and maintain the semblance of order! Couldn't she just do better? Try harder? It wasn't rocket science. It didn't take a genius to figure out that when things were a constant disaster-zone, important stuff got misplaced!

Lance threw his truck into reverse and kicked up gravel as he ripped out of the drive. He drove too fast, but with his pulse racing and all the unspoken frustration and arguments flying around his head, the only outlet for that energy at the moment was through the bottom of his right foot.

He punched Cody's number and waited for his foreman to answer.

"Hey boss, how's it going?"

No time for small talk, Lance cut to the chase,

"We've got a problem. Check the permits for the house on Riverside. Is it county or city?"

"What's wrong? Did we pull the wrong permit?"

He adjusted his grip on the steering wheel and spoke louder, "Just look at the stupid paper, Cody."

"Okay, okay. Hold your horses. Let me find it." Lance heard the rustling of papers. He knew exactly where the permit would be and so did Cody. They had a system they used at every jobsite. An impromptu visit by an inspector? Step this way, here's everything you need. How hard was that? After a moment, Cody spoke again. "Okay, found it. Looks like the permit is from the county. What's going on?"

Lance felt his blood pressure rise.

"Okay, here's the deal. We've got a problem with the county, and I need you to shut down the site. I'll contact the homeowners, and I'm going to sort this out." This was his biggest job, and Lance promised them he'd be done by Christmas. Plus, there were still two more ongoing projects to check. One of them he was pretty sure was city, but he couldn't remember if the other was within city limits.

"What is going on?"

"I can't talk about it right now; just shut it down and clean up. Then," he continued after considering, "have the crew head over and help Jason at the house on Rocky Trail Road." Lance pinched the bridge of his nose. "While you are there, come up with something for me to do, preferably something that involves a sledgehammer." He needed to break something. Didn't they have a bathroom to demolish or something? Maybe circa-1960 yellow porcelain tile or cheap, discolored kitchen cabinets.

"Sledgehammer, eh? Did Renovation Barbie break your heart, boss?" Lance cringed at the nickname he had given Daisy. One of many nicknames, actually. Disaster Daisy. Messy Jessie. Calamity Jane. That was before he knew her, though. Before he'd kissed her. Held her while she cried.

Lance hung up on his friend. He didn't want to think about Daisy right now. Just minutes ago, he had walked out on her. Moments before that, they'd been kissing in the kitchen. Everything inside him was screaming to reach out to her, but she was the entire reason he was in this mess, and for now, he couldn't get past that. Instead, he called his other two site leaders. The Rocky Trail project was okay to continue, but the other was on a county permit and had to shut down as well.

Exactly what he did not need.

Lance hadn't been drumming up business or

scheduling new projects because he'd been so busy at Bloom's Farm. Now, he was paying for it. That's what he got for putting his personal wants ahead of the long-term success and stability of the company.

He wouldn't make that mistake again.

Lance had to get the permits unsuspended, and if that obnoxious inspector had his way, it wouldn't be easy. The guy had practically crowed about shutting down Matthews Construction, obviously loving making Lance squirm. What was with him, anyway?

The inspector had to have some stake in this whole situation, or he wouldn't waste his time investigating bogus complaints, especially after Lance had disproven every single one of them. He'd spent hours walking the inspector through the building, showing him each complaint was patently false. Yet, he'd come back again, digging for more. Havershem had finally found a chink in the armor and delivered a direct blow.

There was more to the story. No doubt it was linked to the mysterious internet bullies. Whoever it was, they'd done a thorough job. Daisy had no earthly idea where her permits were, and even if she miraculously found them, the inspector could stall the verification as long he wanted to.

Frustration surged as he thought how easily this

could have been prevented— if Daisy had just been more organized. Lance adjusted his baseball hat and pulled it firmly back down. The whole situation was a disaster.

Yeah, a sledgehammer definitely sounded like a good idea.

19

Two hours later, papers crumpled loudly and small receipts fell to the floor as Daisy rifled feverishly through every stack of paperwork she could find.

Every scrap of paper in the kitchen and living room had already been searched, and she was pouring through every inch of her bedroom. If Daisy didn't find the permit in here, Hawthorne's room was next. It didn't matter if there was no logical explanation for it to be in his room—enough years of misplaced jewelry, sweaters, cellphones, and retainers had taught her that logic wasn't usually a factor when it came to her tendency to lose things.

Daisy had definitely pulled all the correct

permits, a mistake narrowly prevented by Greg when he started working with her.

But where on God's green earth was her copy of the permit? The previous inspector had signed it when he inspected the new support beams and then again when she and Lance finished all the electrical work.

Daisy gasped. She remembered it perfectly now! Lance had handed the signed permit to her after her jubilant celebratory hug.

With a wink, she had tucked it inside the roof of her hardhat, and said, "For safekeeping." It had taken her a few stressful minutes too long to find it ahead of that inspection, and Daisy didn't want to lose it again.

Daisy tore down the stairs, desperate to find her pink hardhat—a gift from Lance's father—and the critical paperwork held within.

This new inspector was on an absolute power trip. What had happened to the other guy? He was nice. He never threatened them or made Daisy want to practice her aerobic kickboxing moves on his squishy frame.

Finally, after looking in every room at least twice, Daisy found her hardhat, mostly buried in a box of packing peanuts. How on earth had it gotten there?

With a silent prayer, Daisy flipped over the hardhat and felt a wave of relief when she spotted the yellow carbon copied document.

Carefully, she pulled it out and gingerly unfolded it. There it was, only one signature line remaining for final inspection. Hallelujah!

Unfortunately, this was only half the battle. Maybe not even that much of it. A quarter.

The real challenge would be convincing the power-tripping Mr. Havershem to approve them to start work again. He seemed determined to delay their progress, no matter what she did.

And Lance's other projects, too.

Now that she had the permit in hand, she had to face the reality that her careless attitude had caused real consequences. Not just for her, either, but for someone who had only ever been helpful to her.

And where did that get him? Out of work for two weeks through no fault of his own. What could she do? Since the beginning, they had both agreed they were all wrong for each other. Now, she had practically ruined his business—and her own!

Why would he want to spend his life permanently attached to someone like her? The last few weeks, Lance had been the only bright spot in a whirlwind of hospital visits and anxiety-laced prayers. For some inexplicable reason, Lance had readily shouldered her burden after Thanksgiving. Since then, they'd grown closer every day.

Her mom always said Daisy would lose her own feet if they weren't attached! With the events of the day in retrospect, it was probably a pretty accurate statement. Lance was probably realizing what a mistake it had been to enter a relationship with her. They were too different; being together could only frustrate him and cause more trouble. Daisy knew how important his business was to him, and Lance didn't deserve to have it threatened because of her carelessness.

No, Lance was definitely better off without her. Even if it sucked to admit it to herself. Would she be okay without him, though? She couldn't decide if being with Lance forever would be the best thing that ever happened to her, or if he would slowly suck the spirit out of her. It seemed an awfully big risk to take. It didn't matter though, because being with her would mean nothing but trouble for him.

The project was close enough now that she could finish it herself with Hawthorne's help. And Andi said she would be home for two weeks at Christmas. Daisy could bribe her to help.

It was time to put Lance out of his misery. He'd

only taken on her project as a favor to his dad anyway. He wouldn't mind.

She did need to straighten things out at the county though, and make sure he and his business didn't suffer the consequences for her carelessness. The idea that everything Lance had worked so hard for would be ruined because of her made her sick to her stomach.

She texted him, ignoring the sting of tears in her eyes.

Found the permits. I promise I'll fix it. I'm fine, don't worry about coming back.

There. Letting him off the hook was the right move. Now, she just had to convince her heart.

20

*D*aisy paced anxiously in the atrium of the Indianapolis Airport, glancing down the hallway every few moments. She looked for any sign of her sister in the stream of people coming toward them, pulling tiny suitcases on impossibly small wheels.

"Daisy, relax. She'll get here when she gets here," Lily patted Daisy's shoulder reassuringly, but Daisy shrugged it off.

Andi was getting closer. Somehow, she could feel it. Her heart lifted inexplicably.

Andi was here!

Daisy stepped on a bench to get a better view and spotted her sister, sporting desert-sand army fatigues and a short pixie-style haircut.

Her heart soared and Daisy waved enthusiastically, meeting Andi's gaze. Her sister smiled and rolled her eyes. "There she is, guys!"

Everyone stood and unfolded their signs. "Welcome Home, Andi!" and "All I want for Christmas is my sister home." Hawthorne held balloons and a giant picture he'd printed of a dandelion. Always a smart aleck.

They made quite a sight among the stream of people talking busily on cellphones in their business suits.

Finally, Andi was beyond the security guard, and Daisy ran to her. Andi's giant, brown duffel bag hit the floor as the two sisters embraced. Travelers in the airport stopped and clapped as they watched the reunion. Embarrassingly, Daisy started to cry, and she tried to wipe the tears on scratchy patches on her sister's shoulders.

"Hey, Daze," Andi said with a quiet chuckle, "Miss me?"

"Not even a smidge, big sister," Daisy sniffled. "But I'm sure glad you're here now." There was something Daisy couldn't explain about having her sister so far away. There always a piece of her tied up in knots with worry. It started immediately upon hanging up from one of their video chats, gradually ratcheting tighter and tighter until she saw her sister's face again through the screen. Even then, she never fully relaxed until she held Andi in her arms. Daisy kept a hand on Andi's arm as they walked back to the rest of the family.

Andi smiled and hugged each sibling in turn. Until she got to Hawthorne and his dandelion sign, which she responded to by putting a hand on her hip and staring him down. He smirked and asked, "What?"

"Hawthorne Bloom." The warning in her voice was clear.

Hawthorne didn't know when to quit. "Dandelion Bloom," he mimicked.

Andi faked a punch to his gut and gave him a firm tap on the head when he curled to protect it. He laughed and handed the sign to Poppy before wrapping Andi up in a hug.

"It is so good to see you guys!" Andi said. "How's Dad?"

Lily had officially become the family spokesperson, answering that question when people called or stopped by with casseroles. "He's doing better. They've got him in a rehab facility for another few days, but he should be home for Christmas. Physically, he's doing quite well, but the stroke impacted his speech and mental function."

Daisy had been amazed to find her dad walking around his room with a walker at the rehabilitation facility. He had brightened at seeing her, but Daisy's heart broke when he soon became agitated and angry. Daisy's mom seemed to think it was because he recognized everyone, but could not remember or say their names. "Mom wanted to be here with us, but she didn't think she should leave Dad."

Andi nodded firmly, "I understand. I want to go see him first thing."

Their large group moved through the round atrium and went to baggage claim to get Andi's things.

"Seriously, you guys couldn't bring two cars?" Andi asked from the middle seat of the second row of their mom's SUV.

"Lavender insisted that a road trip would be fun," Daisy chimed in.

"What?" exclaimed Lavender. "I volunteered to drive my car with three people so we wouldn't have to be so packed." Daisy gave a sheepish smile. Okay, it had been her who talked the group into cramming into one vehicle.

"Oh, get over it. It's good for the environment, right Poppy?"

Poppy nodded. "As the hippie in the family, I officially approve."

"Well, as the old person in the family, I officially do not," Lily said.

"What do you have to complain about? You're riding shotgun," Hawthorne pouted. "I'm the one back here with my knees jammed to my chest." Daisy glanced back to Hawthorne in the third row and stifled a laugh. He did look pretty uncomfortable.

"Who's hungry?" Daisy yelled, changing the subject. They pulled through Andi's choice of fast-food restaurant. She always complained about not having it while deployed.

They ate their food and talked on the drive to Terre Haute to see their dad. This would be the first time their dad had seen everyone at the same time. She prayed it would go well and not overwhelm him.

Would they even all fit in his tiny room? Turns out, she didn't need to worry about it, because her mom greeted them at the door and walked the group to a community room. They passed a frail woman in a wheelchair, sitting slumped to one side. There was a younger man, with two broken legs, who looked angry with the world.

Overall, it was a pretty depressing place. There were so many people in pain and unable to care for themselves. Nurses moved quietly, their white sneakers padding on carpet and tile alike, their brightly colored scrubs adding small splashes of color to the dull interior design. Her father didn't belong in a place like this. It wasn't a nursing home, but it was hard to equate it to anything else.

Her father wasn't that old, was he?

Daisy's mom and dad walked slowly through the doors, her father using his walker with each step and Laura staying inches from his side, encouraging quietly.

Daisy and her siblings were quiet, watching their father struggle. Only a month ago, he'd been baling hay and riding horses. When Dad finally reached the armchair they'd left open for him in the small seating arrangement, he sat down with a loud sigh. He grinned, looking around the room at all of them together.

First, he looked at Hawthorne, and lifted a finger, "Haa-Haath," he stuttered, looking to his wife for confirmation.

"Yes, that's Hawthorne."

Her dad's eyes moved to meet Daisy's own and he said "Da-Day" and she grinned in response. This was amazing progress!

When he reached Andi in the circle of his children, Keith's eyes began to water and he opened his arms wide. "Da-dan?" Frustrated, he tried again. "Dan-dee. Lahh?"

Andi stepped forward and kneeled in front of him, "Hi Dad. You're right, it's me, Dandelion." He sighed in relief that he had conveyed her name and she reached in to hug him.

Daisy felt the tears on her cheeks and laughed, wiping them away. Her twin pulled back from the hug and said, "Andi will be fine." Her parents had always insisted on using Andi's full name, much to her chagrin.

The entire group erupted with laughter when their father shook his head. "Dah. Dee-lah."

Andi relented and laid her head in her dad's lap. "Okay, Dad. You can call me Dandelion."

21

*L*ance carefully positioned his nail gun on the baseboard and squeezed the trigger. Well, it was Cody's nail gun, because his was still at Bloom's Farm. He couldn't bring himself to go back to pick them up. He had walked out on Daisy, and with every errant thought of her, Lance was regretting it. Daisy's text message had stung, but he was also relieved she wasn't waiting for him. He was still so upset he wasn't sure what he would say. Work at Rocky Trail was way ahead of schedule since his entire crew had been working there for a full week, instead of spread out at two other jobs.

It was too many people, and he'd already sent home the subcontractors. But his main crew? They needed work. It was the holidays and the last thing he wanted to do was send them home without a paycheck. As a child, Christmas cheer tended to ebb and flow with the construction economy. While he couldn't overcome the cyclic nature of the market, Lance would do everything possible to ensure his business was consistent and viable. Which is why he'd spent so many years building up a base of repeat clients and a solid referral business.

Of course, having to completely stop work on two projects right before the holidays was potentially devastating to his reputation. One of the clients was an investor who, while he hadn't been happy, knew Lance would do everything in his power to fix it. Quickly.

The other wasn't being quite so understanding. They'd already threatened to bring in another contractor to finish the job and to tell all their friends about the negative experience. Lance had an appointment at the county tomorrow with a friend who could hopefully work things out. If he couldn't? Lance was in a heap of trouble. His business was comfortable and he had decent savings, but he couldn't afford to keep paying his crews if the jobs started disappearing. Daisy said she would fix it, but he wasn't going to hold his breath.

Cody positioned the next piece of trim and

Lance shot three nails along the length to secure it. "Where's your head today, boss?"

Lance glanced at him and shot another nail, "Huh?"

"I said, where's your head at? Because it definitely isn't here."

Lance shook his head, "I know, I'm sorry. I'm still struggling with this whole permit issue. I've worked my tail off for ten years to build this business. And now? Everything comes to a complete halt because Daisy couldn't keep track of a stupid piece of paper."

"Is that all?"

"Of course it is." Lance rankled at the question. What else could there be? His company was being threatened, and it wasn't his fault.

Of course, that's probably how Daisy felt too. But it wasn't the same. Her business wasn't even up and running yet. Matthews Construction was his livelihood. After growing up with a single parent and lean times often overshadowing the better? He couldn't stand to see his business struggle.

"If you say so," his friend responded.

Cody was probably right. It wasn't just the business. It was Daisy, too. And the fact that he wanted simultaneously to wring her neck and beg for forgiveness. Lance sighed. "Sorry, I'm not trying to be difficult." He stood and stretched. "I think I'm going to take off. You're right, I'm probably doing more harm than good being here." Lance said goodbye and headed to his truck, unsure of where to go.

Lance drove without a destination, surprised when he found himself on his father's street. He pulled into the driveway and made his way up the familiar wooden steps he'd climbed as a child.

"Dad?" he called as he walked in.

"Lance, is that you?" his dad responded before peeking his head around the corner. "Hey, son. Was I expecting you?"

Lance waved a hand before pulling off his boots and coat. "No, it was a spur-of-the-moment thing."

With a smile his dad replied, "Well then, alright. Come on in."

"How's your knee?"

His dad hobbled down the hallway ahead of him. "Oh, it's alright. Already better than it was before surgery, it seems. Even though I have to use this blasted cane everywhere I go." When they settled in the living room, his father's eyes turned to him. "So, are you going to tell me what's going on, or do I have to torture it out of you?"

Lance smiled weakly and pulled off his baseball hat. "Have you heard from Daisy at all?"

A wrinkle formed on his father's forehead. "No, not since before Thanksgiving. Why?"

Lance started to explain how after Thanksgiving he and Daisy became something more than friends. His dad's glee was barely disguised. When he explained about the inspector stopping by and harassing them, anger flashed on his dad's face.

"That seems ridiculous," Greg slapped the arm of the chair.

"The kicker is that last time, he asked for Daisy's permit. She, of course, couldn't find it and he shut the whole thing down."

Greg winced. "Yikes. I bet Daisy was fired up about that."

"I'm sure she was, but I was a little preoccupied. Because he shut me down, too. All my jobsites where the permit was county-issued."

His dad's eyes grew wide. "I've never heard of the county doing that before. The permits are basically a formality. This isn't Indianapolis!"

Lance agreed and he told him his plans to meet with his friend tomorrow. "It's really bad, Dad. I've got crews to pay, and they can't work, which means I can't get paid. Everything I've spent my career working for is about to disappear and I'm kind of freaking out about it."

"Hey, hey, calm down. It's going to be okay, you know that, right?"

Lance shook his head, "Easy for you to say. You didn't see how giddy this guy was to shut down my projects. He's not backing down that easily."

"It doesn't matter. You are forgetting something you should have learned a long time ago."

Lance raised his eyebrows and waited.

"You're forgetting who is really in control. It isn't the inspector, and it sure as heck isn't you." His dad leaned forward and rested his elbows on his knees. "God's got this. And until you start trusting Him instead of yourself, you are going to be miserable."

Stunned, Lance sat back against the couch. Was his dad right? Was Lance trying to control everything instead of trusting God? He prayed, and he read his Bible. Well, sometimes at least.

"I'm speaking from experience, son. I can't tell you how many times God had to teach me this same lesson when you were young."

What was it like while Lance was growing up? "How did you do it?"

His dad laughed lightly, "I didn't have much of a choice. You were everything to me, and trying to provide a good life for you took everything I had—

and more. The only way I made it was by recognizing that God is good, and He had it handled."

A quiet moment passed before Lance spoke
again. "I'm not sure how to do that."

Leaning back in the chair, his dad replied, "Well,
a good place to start is to ask Him to help you figure
it out."

Maybe his dad was onto something. There was
no one Lance admired more than the man who sacri-
ficed everything to raise him. It seemed impossible,
though. Every muscle within him was screaming to
fix it and scolding him for dropping the ball and
being irresponsible. It was up to him to save his
company, because it was his own fault it was in trouble. Daisy may have lost the permit, but he lost focus
on his goals.

Was it wrong to think he could control it? Did
God really care about his little home renovation
company anyway? Deep inside, the answer came—
God loved him, which meant God cared about what
he cared about.

If his dad was right and Lance needed to give
control to God, it wasn't going to be easy. Lance was
a self-proclaimed control-freak. Despite his father's
dedication, his underlying fear of instability came
from being abandoned by his mother and being a

financial burden on his father. He never wanted that instability again.

He couldn't guarantee insecurity would never come though. There was always the potential for business to dry up—the market could tank tomorrow. Or, he could get sick and all his finances be dumped into medical bills and prescriptions. The barrage of potential problems terrified him. Lance had worked his entire life to create a safety net. But it would never be big enough, even if he won the lottery. Money couldn't save him.

Lance said a distracted farewell and went back to his truck.

Maybe his dad was right. Lance needed something bigger than the problems of this world. He needed to trust in the God he professed to believe in. It seemed a funny thing that belief and trust could be so closely linked, but feel so radically different.

Lance believed in Jesus, but he had never truly trusted God with the details of his life. He was too busy trying to control it himself. That needed to change—starting now.

22

*L*ance needed to retrieve the tools he'd left behind at the farm, but he hadn't worked up the courage. He didn't really need them anyway, with only one project ongoing. His friend at the county hadn't had any luck in clearing the gridlock with the permits.

Despite his frustration with Daisy, if she looked at him and asked him to come back, he was ninety percent sure he would agree. The other ten percent was waffling, despite the inner voice repeatedly reminding him why he left.

Lance pulled up to his dad's house on Christmas Eve, surprised to see an unfamiliar car in the drive. Who was here? Christmas Eve was usually just him and his Dad and the candlelight service at church.

With a knock on the door before he opened it, Lance walked in just in time to see his dad jolt out of the embrace of a woman Lance didn't recognize.

His dad blushed and cleared his throat. "Son, is it five o'clock already?" Lance nodded slowly, not taking his eyes from the scene unfolding before him. "Well, I'd like you to meet Marianne. She's the receptionist at the physical therapists' office and," he rubbed the back of his neck, "we sort of hit it off."

Marianne turned to him with a smile, "Hello, Lance. It's so nice to finally meet you."

"Is it?" Lance didn't begrudge his father happiness. In fact, several times in his teens and twenties he'd tried to encourage his dad to date. But he never had. This was unexpected, that was all. Guilt twinged at his unkind greeting and he tried again. "Marianne, I'm glad you're here. Will you be joining us for church tonight?"

"Oh, yes. That was the plan. Then I will skedaddle so I can set out milk and cookies with my grandchildren before they go to bed." Marianne gave a warm smile and Lance couldn't help but return it. His dad was dating a grandmother—interesting. Was his dad really old enough to be dating a grandma? It was a sobering thought.

With a new lens, he studied his father. His dad

was fit, still athletic and lean as ever. The short-trimmed hair that remained was admittedly more salt than pepper these days. Wrinkles creased around his dad's eyes, all the more evident from the broad smile he wore watching Lance and Marianne interact.

Greg rubbed his hands together in excitement, "This is just fantastic, isn't it? I'll go grab a clean shirt, and we can head out. Service starts at 5:30!"

Lance made small talk with Marianne while they waited, asking about her children and her job at the rehab clinic. She was very nice, but it was still weird. He had a feeling it would be uncomfortable for a while. Lance's mom left thirty years ago. That was a long time with just the two of them. The two musketeers.

It was refreshing to see his dad so excited. The last time he'd been this excited, he'd been starting work on the Bloom homestead.

There it was again. Everything these days brought Lance back to thoughts about Daisy and Bloom's Farm. It was ridiculous. The last thing he needed was to dwell on the Heartbreak Hotel and the beautiful and incredibly charming owner.

Trying to convince the piece of him still clinging to thoughts of Daisy, Lance had tried to recreate the wishlist he'd made years ago with qualities he wanted in a wife. He even tried praying about the list before he made it. Which had been a bad idea, because a twinge of conviction hit every time he tried to write things like 'organized' on the list.

Frustrated, he had crumpled up the empty paper and tossed it toward the trashcan. It was a stupid idea anyway.

His dad came down and they headed out. Lance was driving himself while his dad climbed in with Marianne, the slight limp barely noticeable as he opened her door and walked around the rear of the car to the passenger seat, flashing Lance a thumbs up.

Christmas Eve service was busy, and parking was scarce. Finally, Lance grabbed a spot and walked to the lobby. There were Christmas cookies out, and children ran around the foyer in velvet dresses and button-down shirts.

He spotted his dad and Marianne and made his way through the crowd. "Wow, quite a turn out," Lance commented. "Shall we head in?" What happened to the somber, quiet Christmas Eve he remembered as a kid? He was eager to escape the chaos of the lobby and enter the sanctuary, hopefully quieter and more peaceful.

As Lance sat through the service, his thoughts kept circling back to Daisy. Andi was home, right? It would be fun to see them together. How different would they be? What would Andi think of him? The thoughts stalled right there. Why did it matter what Andi thought of him? Surely, it was the same as Daisy.

Actually, what did Daisy think of him?

They'd kissed more than a few times after Thanksgiving. Other than a few disagreements, they'd fallen into a comfortable routine of flirting and working and laughing. In every aspect, it had been a relationship—a really good one.

Then? The inspector.

Lance tensed despite the familiar, soothing music. The last visit from the inspector derailed everything. If only Daisy had found the paperwork!

He kept coming back to this. Was she right for him or not? His heart screamed yes, but his head hollered a firm no, reminding him of the misplaced tools and haphazard approach. But Lance missed her smile and the way she danced to any music she heard, even his ringtone.

Lance knew he was rigid. Cody called him a stick in the mud. Even his dad routinely told him to lighten up and have some fun. But fun didn't pay the bills and laughter didn't finish projects. Too often, fun meant neglecting your responsibilities or your family.

Daisy was fun, though. And she never neglected her family. Not like his mother, who claimed she needed to find herself, disappearing when he was a toddler. No, Daisy would never do that. Her sense of loyalty to her family ran deep. He'd seen it in how she talked about Andi and how she cared for her father. Daisy had loved her brother when he bailed after Keith's stroke. Daisy might not be organized or boring, but she was rock solid when it came to standing with her family.

Could that be enough? Daisy might not leave like his mother had, but she was still a tornado he wasn't sure how to tame—if it was even possible. If he just had some reassurance that she could do better and try harder, maybe they could make it work. Maybe he could help her get organized.

Instead of listening to the Pastor talk about the gift of God's love, Lance rationalized with God. If God would show him how to help Daisy wrangle some of her Disaster Daisy tendencies, Lance would do it.

The only question remaining was whether Daisy would let him help.

23

*A*ndi leaned over, grabbing Daisy's phone from her hand, "I can't believe he texted you last night,"

"Hey, that's mine!" Sometimes sisters were so annoying.

"Just let me read it. You know you'll tell me everything anyway. This will just save us time," Andi said, and Daisy sat back with a frown. It was probably true, but that didn't mean she was happy about being bossed around.

Andi was staying in one of the finished guest suites, since Daisy had filled her construction downtime by assembling furniture and decorating. It was still early on Christmas morning and soon they needed to go up to the main house for brunch.

They'd tried to talk Mom out of it, but she'd insisted. Weekly brunch hadn't been a priority with Dad in rehab. Thankfully, he came home two days ago. Christmas was an honorary Saturday anyway, made for all-day pajamas and cocoa. And in the Bloom Family? Brunch.

Andi's mouth fell open and Daisy closed her eyes. Andi was reading the text message. The one that had her twisted up in knots and had followed polite but impersonal Christmas wishes.

"I can't believe he said this!" Andi quoted the message. "I miss you, Daisy. I would love to see you again and see where things go from there." She looked up from the phone, "What is he thinking?"

Daisy shook her head and grabbed the phone. "I don't know. The man can't make up his mind. First, we should date. Then, we are all wrong. Then, we should try again. Then the inspector shuts everything down and he bails!" It was infuriating. Of course, it didn't help that Daisy was in exactly the same place, unable to decide if losing her heart to Lance would crush her spirit or make her happy. Or if it was even fair to him to be stuck with her.

Maybe she just needed to talk to him, like he said. Maybe they could work it out. She was still trying to fix the whole inspector issue.

Daisy didn't know how much impact it was having on his business, but it definitely couldn't be good. It was an unplanned schedule snafu, and Lance didn't do well with unpredictability. Which was unfortunate, because Daisy's existence was almost entirely composed of forgetfulness, rescheduling, and misadventures.

That was a very big reason they were all wrong for each other, despite the obvious chemistry and the sizzling kisses.

Deciding to ignore that particular text message for today, they headed over for the Christmas celebration. Daisy caught her mom in the kitchen for a rare moment alone, she hugged her deeply, reveling in the comfortable embrace of someone who loved her unconditionally.

"I love you, Mom."

"I love you too, Daisy girl."

"You doing okay?" She studied her mom, seeing new wrinkles between her eyebrows and gray hairs streaking her mom's natural blond, only noticeable if you looked closely.

Mom gave her a kind smile, genuine but strained. "I'm okay. It's been hard, but I know God's got me. What about you?"

Daisy glanced toward the living room, her eyes

instinctively finding Andi in the midst of the group. "I'm good. I'm just glad Andi is here. Everything has been so crazy with the B&B and the whole thing with Lance just—"

"What's going on with the B&B?" her mom asked.

Daisy told her about the inspector and the negative reviews.

"Oh, I'm so sorry I didn't even know, Daisy! Do you need me to reach out to some friends?"

Daisy shook her head. Her mom's willingness to help was not unexpected. "No, but thank you. I've got this." Her mom had enough on her plate.

"I understand, but if you change your mind, let me know. Now tell me more about this Lance. What's going on there?"

How much should she tell her mom? "Well, you know Greg had his knee replaced and couldn't work on the house anymore. His son took over the project, which was fine. Except, he is completely frustrating. Lance is rigid and controlling. He makes endless lists and cleans things up all the time." Daisy felt her words getting away from her as the complaints starting rolling off her tongue faster and faster. "Oh, and his stupid systems." Daisy spit out the word. "And then he goes and kisses me in the crawlspace

—" Laura's eyebrows shot to the ceiling and Daisy gasped and covered her mouth. Whoops, did not mean to mention that.

"Come again?" her mom asked.

"Well, he sort of... kissed me. Then we decided we weren't right for each other. It's been this whole thing. And I definitely do not want to talk about it." Daisy shut down the conversation and ignored the surprise on her mom's face. Rose walked in, asking her mom a question and providing the perfect distraction. Time to duck back into the living room.

Daisy walked to the over-sized armchair, and her twin moved to make room without looking away from the television. It had always been that way between them—no words necessary.

This Christmas looked radically different from any before. With Dad just moved back home and Mom doing everything she could just to hold it together, Christmas decorations fell down the priority list. At least Lily put up a tree a few days ago, with help from Rose and Lavender.

Instead of her dad's usual attempts to get everyone singing along to Christmas carols, Keith sat in the corner of the couch, in festive pajama pants two sizes too big after the weight he'd lost in the hospital. But he was home.

Thirty minutes later, after they all filed into the kitchen, her mom asked Hawthorne to pray. Usually her dad prayed before big meals, but he still couldn't speak clearly.

Hawthorne gave thanks for their father being home and for their mother's love and devotion. Andi squeezed Daisy's hand three times in the silent signal from when they were kids: thankful for you.

When Hawthorne finished, they passed dishes of food around the table. It had been four weeks since their last family brunch, but it felt like a lifetime.

"You know, we need to start up Saturday brunches now that Dad is back home," Daisy said.

"Absolutely," Lavender said.

"I'll help cook," Lily offered, silencing the objections their mother was starting to add.

"Yeah, I know we all live and work around here, but I still miss you guys," Hawthorne said.

"Awww! Girls, did you hear that? He likes us! He really likes us!" Poppy folded her hands together in front of her chest, mocking their brother's uncharacteristic soft side and laughter broke out around the dining room.

The gifts that often tempted families to let them become the center of the celebration became secondary to the joy at the Bloom house today. It had been a long, painful, exhausting month for each of them. There were things that had happened Daisy could only recall as a blur of activity. Since Thanksgiving, they'd pulled together in a way she hadn't honestly known they could.

Hawthorne stepped up, big time. Daisy glanced at Avery and smiled, so grateful for the friendship they'd rekindled. Poppy was still keeping whatever was going on with Harrison completely under wraps, but Daisy knew her sister was there for her one-hundred percent.

That's what family was for.

24

*A*ndi's visit was over in a flash. After Andi cleared out of the guest room, Daisy made a list of everything left to get the bed-and-breakfast ready.

Diet Dr. Pepper and a purple pen in hand, Daisy sat at the small bistro table in the kitchen—the same table where she dreamed up the bed-and-breakfast before any of the construction even started. It was also where she and Lance debated project priorities and shared protein bar lunches or the occasional gas station pizza.

Daisy glanced around, studying the kitchen. Bright cabinets and open wood shelving contrasted nicely with the large commercial appliances she had insisted on. In the dining room, through large French doors, a rustic, farm-style table dominated the space, providing bench seating for twelve or more. With some centerpieces and pretty place settings, it would be the perfect place for gourmet breakfasts.

The to-do list was growing. Daisy wrote a few completed items and checked them off for the sole satisfaction of having them marked out. *What is happening?* Daisy wasn't a list maker, yet here she was—voluntarily making one and following it. Lance would be proud.

Draining the last sweet sips of her soda, Daisy stood and tossed the empty can into the trash can across the room. When it missed, she considered leaving it where it lay. Instead, she walked over and placed it in the trash.

The top priority on her list was emptying the bedrooms and painting. She'd lived here for about a year and thought she was living pretty sparsely. Yet, the process of packing revealed more things had accumulated than she thought.

In fact, she found an entire box of knickknacks and decorations in the back of her closet, buried under a pile of not-quite-dirty-but-not-quite-clean clothes. Daisy had picked up the items at a thrift store and promptly forgot about them. They would be perfect for the mantle in the parlor.

There was still so much to do, though. And without a contractor, would she complete everything? It seemed impossible to get the bed-and-breakfast finished in time to open before the busy spring and summer travel season.

This was her dream, and it was getting harder every step of the way. First Greg and his knee. Then the reviews. The inspector. The work-stop order. If God wanted Daisy to start a bed-and-breakfast, He sure had a funny way of showing it!

Daisy wandered through the house, examining the familiar features she loved. The mantle in the parlor had been a weekend project she tackled on her own, sanding and staining the beautiful, solid wood piece.

In the living room, boxes of supplies and the temporary workbench still cluttered the space. Her eyes fell on Lance's drill and other small power tools. Surely, he needed those. Or maybe he didn't, because he couldn't work on his other projects?

With a sigh, Daisy found an empty box and gathered the tools, grabbing his screwdrivers, drill bits, extra batteries, and hammer. At some point, Lance would want his tools back. Better to get them ready now.

Were some of his things still upstairs? Just to be

sure, Daisy jogged up the stairs and took a pass through the bedrooms, hallway, and bathrooms. The only thing she found was a pair of safety goggles and a flashlight under the sink in the blue bathroom. It was the last major project on their list.

She turned the goggles over in her hands, remembering the first day he came to work, when he lectured her about worksite safety. There were repeated moments after when he'd reminded her again with a wordless tap of his finger on his own glasses. Daisy usually rolled her eyes but lowered her goggles from her head to her nose. Lance always waited to turn on the saw or drill until she was protected.

Maybe he was more patient than she gave him credit for.

Daisy glanced around the blue bathroom with a sigh. It was a daunting task to tackle. If it didn't get done though, it would be the most memorable thing about the bed-and-breakfast—and not in a good way. The online trolls would have a heyday if she booked reservations and guests used the atrocious 60s bathroom.

It had been over a month since Daisy looked online for reviews. Lavender hadn't been too forthcoming about anything she'd seen. Part of Daisy wanted to stick her head in the sand and ignore the internet entirely. The other part needed to read every single word that had ever been written about her inn.

Daisy pulled her phone out and dismissed a few unimportant notifications. Her thumb hovered over the internet app, and finally tapped the button, pulling up a blank, white page with an empty search bar in the center.

Should she? Could she handle it right now?

The temptation to check the web for mention of Bloom's Farm Bed and Breakfast was too great, and Daisy finally typed her own business name into the search bar.

Results flooded the page in familiar blue ink. Sponsored ads dominated the top, websites declaring they could provide the best deals on booking a room. She scrolled to find websites splashed with the reviews she'd already seen. Do not stay here! Terribly disappointing. Waste of money. It was her worst nightmare. In the words hiding behind blurry eyes, Daisy saw yet another one of her dreams going up in smoke, due to something she couldn't control.

Was God playing some sort of cruel joke on her?

Daisy clicked through to a website she knew featured reviews on all types of businesses. Reading each lengthy review bashing her beloved project threw her deeper into self-pity with a healthy dose of anger.

Daisy had watched one dream die, her professional dancing days ending far too soon. It had taken years before she uncovered a dream buried in the potential of the old, weathered homestead. The house had come so far; it was on the verge of being something incredible. All she needed to do was redo this bathroom and wrap up a few smaller projects downstairs.

Could she do it on her own, though?

Only one way to find out.

First step? She had to get this ridiculous permit issue resolved. But Christmas had given her an idea. That's what family was for, right?

DAISY BROUGHT backup for her meeting with the inspector. Poppy was her ace-in-the-hole; everybody loved her. Plus, other than their father, Poppy had the most influence because of her produce operation and orchard events. She'd turned their small farm into something of a tourist attraction and worked with the county on multiple occasions for special permits.

When the polite secretary led them into a small conference room, the inspector greeted them apathetically, except for a small hint of surprise at seeing someone else with Daisy. Poppy smiled with closed lips and pulled her skirt under her to take a seat.

"Let's get started, shall we?" the inspector started. "I understand you aren't happy with—"

Poppy cut him off sweetly, "Let's wait just a moment. I believe we are expecting someone to join us."

The inspector's confused look made Daisy want to dance with glee. He had no idea what was coming and it was glorious.

Just then, the door opened and Daisy recognized Harrison Coulter talking with Gerald Ruiz, the county commissioner. Like old friends, they bantered and laughed as they came through the door. Harrison smiled at Poppy and gave Daisy a nod before greeting the inspector coolly and introducing himself.

Daisy gave Poppy a questioning look. She knew Poppy had called in a favor with the commissioner. But what was Harrison doing here? Poppy mouthed,

"I'll tell you later," before turning back to the stammering inspector.

Gerald came over and Daisy stood to shake his hand. "Miss Bloom, your sister has told me all about you. It's a pleasure to meet an upcoming entrepreneur. Rogers County is eager to help encourage business growth here."

Daisy nodded, "Thank you, sir. Unfortunately, the process hasn't included as much... support from the county as I'd hoped." She glanced across the table.

Gerald frowned and looked at Mr. Havershem, "What's she talking about, Larry?"

Larry sputtered, "I'm not sure, Mr. Ruiz. I assure you—"

Daisy rolled her eyes and tried to stifle the simmering frustration.

Harrison's confident voice cut through the inspector's protests. "From my understanding, your inspector has been intentionally placing roadblocks to prevent Miss Bloom here from successfully completing her project. As someone deeply involved in the Indiana Senate Committee for Economic Development, I have to say this is very disappointing. Small businesses are the heart of the economy, and we should do everything in our power to aid," he glanced at Mr. Havershem, "not hinder, their progress."

Gerald nodded enthusiastically, "I couldn't agree more, Senator. I can assure you, we here at Rogers County place small business success as a very high priority."

Daisy snorted. "You should probably tell Mr. Havershem over there."

The commissioner frowned at Larry. "What's going on?"

Larry's face turned bright red and he sputtered. "There were complaints and I—"

Poppy chimed in, "Bogus complaints, Mr. Commissioner."

Harrison laid a hand on Poppy's shoulder, and Daisy's eyes widened at the familiarity. "I had my people do a little digging, and I am confident there has been an egregious conflict of interest by Mr. Havershem."

Gerald narrowed his eyebrows, "Why don't you explain now, before I have to hear it from the esteemed Senator?"

Larry stood up, pushing his pudgy hands into the table. "My sister runs a bed-and-breakfast only five miles away from Bloom's Farm! This will destroy her business, and what was I supposed to do? Just let this harpy ruin everything she'd worked for?"

Daisy gasped at his insult, "Excuse me?"

Spittle flew from Larry's mouth when he spoke, "Oh, I saw you with that contractor, practically falling all over him. Absolutely shameless." Daisy's eyes bugged, and she felt heat travel up her neck to her cheeks in embarrassment and anger. This guy was unbelievable.

Before Daisy could muster the words to tear him down, Poppy came to her defense and Harrison practically had to hold Daisy's petite-but-feisty younger sister back.

Harrison raised his arm, the other still on Poppy's arm, and spoke over the clash of shouts and accusations. "Enough!" Daisy looked at him with surprise.

Daisy had watched from a distance as he became a city councilman and then State Senator. Seeing him give a press conference was different from seeing him in action though. Harrison definitely commanded respect, and every person in the small conference room immediately obeyed his instruction to sit.

Harrison pulled a chair out for her sister, and

Daisy narrowed her eyes. What on earth had she missed while caught up in her own world?

Harrison turned to the commissioner and spoke firmly, "Gerald, for the sake of the farm's success as a multi-dimensional farm tourism attraction, we need the county to reactivate the permits for Bloom's Farm B&B. And for the projects currently suspended under the contractor..." He glanced at Daisy, "what's his name again?"

"Lance Matthews, Matthews Construction."

"Right. Matthews. He was also unfairly targeted by Larry in an ill-advised attempt to damage the reputation and progress of Bloom's Farm B&B. We also expect the county will take appropriate disciplinary actions against Mr. Havershem for his gross misconduct in this regard."

Daisy watched with awe as a man she hadn't seen in eight years knocked down walls for her. What other explanation could there be except that God was in control? She knew Poppy had been talking to Harrison before Christmas, but beyond that? Nothing to indicate she had this kind of pull with him! What had it taken to for a busy state representative to come to the Rogers County offices to fight her little battle?

Larry tried to speak, but the commissioner held

up a hand to silence him and said, "We will discuss this later. Mr. Coulter—"

"Senator." Harrison corrected and Daisy saw the familiar roll of Poppy's eyes in response to his ego.

"Senator Coulter," Gerald corrected apologetically, "I can assure you this was a mistake and we will do everything in our power to make it right for Miss Bloom and the Bloom Family."

"Wonderful. I guess we are done here. I've got to head back to Indianapolis for a meeting this evening." Harrison stood, and the group followed. Daisy shook Gerald's hand blankly, still trying to process everything.

Her sister swooped in, brought in the man who could be the next Indiana governor, and completely saved the B&B. Daisy now had a pretty good idea who was to blame for her bad reviews. The Butterfly Inn was an ancient B&B not far from Bloom's Farm. It had been around forever and was everything Daisy hated in small private inns. Creepy antique dolls, itchy bedspreads, and too many doilies made you feel like you were in your great aunt's house. She'd actually booked a room when the idea of opening a bed-and-breakfast had first entered her mind.

After a few hours in the room with no television and a particularly unnerving life-sized doll in a rocking chair staring at her from the corner of the room, they had checked out early and went straight home. Lavender had never forgiven her for that particular adventure.

Could all the reviews she'd seen online have come from Larry Havershem's sister? Just because she felt threatened by the competition? Surely there was enough business for both of them, especially with the weddings being held at Bloom's Farm, miles away from the nearest large hotels.

Instead of working together, the owner of Butterfly Inn tried to take her down. Now, the question remained—what was Daisy going to do about it?

Daisy left the meeting with more questions than answers. First and foremost were burning questions for Poppy. Harrison Coulter had shown up at the dinky offices of Rogers County as a personal favor to her sister?

The three of them walked out and Daisy turned to Harrison, "I don't know how to thank you."

Harrison flashed the campaign-winning smile that landed him on the front page of the Indy Star more than once. "It's my pleasure, truly." He glanced at Poppy and then his watch. "I'm sorry, but I really do have to run." Daisy's mouth dropped as he touched Poppy's arm gently and leaned in to kiss her cheek. Color rose in Poppy's cheeks as Harrison whispered something to her before striding away, his phone already halfway to his ear.

The instant they were both in Poppy's truck, Daisy turned to her sister. Poppy stared at the steering wheel, avoiding her gaze.

"Anything you need to tell me, sis?"

Her sister sighed and twisted in the seat. "I meant to tell you a long time ago. Then Dad had his stroke and everything got complicated."

Daisy frowned; it wasn't like her sister to keep secrets. "So, what is it?"

"Harrison and I are...together."

Daisy's gasp filled the small interior of the truck. "Are you serious?" At Poppy's small nod, Daisy covered her mouth. "When?"

"He called in September and asked me to go to a dinner with him. We've been talking and seeing each other since." Poppy's warm brown eyes filled with tears, "I'm so sorry I didn't tell you." Daisy reached across the center console and patted her sister's arm as she continued, "It's been a bit confusing."

No big surprise there. Between their history and the fact that Harrison was in politics? Oh yeah, it could definitely get complicated.

"But you like him?" Watching them at the meeting, Poppy and Harrison hadn't been overtly affectionate. He'd been attentive and stood up for Daisy, but there was the kiss on the cheek before he left.

Poppy bit her lip and nodded. "Yeah. I think you'll be seeing him around a lot more."

Daisy let out a squeal and gave her sister an awkward hug across the console. "I'm so happy for you!" Poppy deserved someone wonderful. Maybe Harrison had been bone-headed in high school, but he'd grown up since then. From everything Daisy saw in the local news, he was a good lawyer and senator. Honestly, it was a bit surprising he wasn't married yet. Last year, there had been a brief flurry on social media when he'd been named one of Indiana's most eligible bachelors. "Thanks for calling in a favor from your influential boyfriend."

They drove back to the farm and Daisy walked into the bed-and-breakfast with renewed energy. She still had to visit the Butterfly Inn and navigate that situation, but the roadblocks to finishing construction were gone. Should she call Lance and let him know?

Calling him would be a bad idea. Her own weakness would probably lead to her begging him for forgiveness and to come finish the job. Daisy couldn't do that to him. Instead, she called the office they'd just left and verified that the county would contact Matthews Construction.

There, her conscience was clear. Almost. She'd never responded to Lance's texts at Christmas two weeks ago. It was still her fault everything had gone down the way it did. It wasn't even all that surprising. Over the years, Daisy had tried every resolution and self-help book on organization. Nothing made a difference. Was she doomed to a life of misplaced cellphones and disappointed boyfriends?

Daisy glanced around her room. Although she'd started packing the other day, dirty laundry was thrown haphazardly across the footboard of the bed. And the back of the chair. And the floor of the closet. Pretty much everywhere except the laundry basket sitting next to the closet door.

She didn't want to live this way; most of the time she barely noticed the clutter. Since working with Lance, the disarray caught her eye more often. As Daisy moved around her room, gathering discarded sweatpants and dirty socks, she hummed quietly.

This bed-and-breakfast opening was a fresh start, in more ways than one. A new dream, a new business. It could be a new leaf for Daisy as well, couldn't it?

She wasn't ready to go as far as Lance, with his

perfectly organized tool box and color-coded socket wrenches. But if Daisy was going to be a successful business woman, she needed to be okay with having a place for important things. She could be somewhat organized and still be herself.

Plus, she had to deal with the owner of The Butterfly Inn. Her first instinct to egg their establishment probably wouldn't be the best approach, even if Rose could probably spare five dozen eggs without a care.

Aunt Jacquie said the desire to fight back had been less important than obeying God's call. No matter how badly Daisy wanted to take out her frustration, it was more important to focus on the call God had given her. Like Aunt Jacquie had done.

Daisy finished tidying her room and continued packing the space, all the while planning how she would go to the neighboring inn and make peace. Now that the permits were cleared, she had a lot of work ahead of her. Unfortunately, the fact that Lance wouldn't be working alongside her made it far less appealing.

25

"Cody, good news! You can head back to Riverside and finish it up."

Finally, Lance was able to get his other jobsites up and running. Actually, he was pretty sure it had been a God thing. Thirty minutes ago, he had gotten a random call from the county saying all the permit issues were completely cleared up. Whatever the reason, Lance was grateful. His own efforts to clear up the situation had been completely stonewalled.

He continued his directions to Cody, "We need to get it wrapped as soon as possible. We're already three weeks behind. So, grab everybody you can and knock it out. I'm serious. Pay the subs extra to move us to the front of the list. Whatever it takes."

Cody was surprised, but Lance knew it was the

right thing to do. There were times when spending a little more was worth it. Keeping your word was one of those times.

Lance was trusting God would take care of the money, and he would focus on running the business with integrity. It was a new approach for him. He'd always operated honestly, but he definitely felt the pressure to drum up business and micromanage everything. These steps of faith in his business weren't coming easily.

Lance still caught himself taking on too much and forcing new business or referrals. But more and more, he was able to feel the nudge of God directing his steps.

In the past, Lance had driven himself into the ground trying to micromanage every transaction and every sheet of drywall. "You've got everything else under control?"

"I got it, Lance," Cody replied. "Trust me, remember?" When he'd talked to Cody about letting go of control, his foreman had been honest, telling Lance he often felt like Lance didn't trust him to do his job.

Which couldn't be further from the truth.

Lance smiled, "Sorry, old habits. Just let me know if you need anything from me." Lance trusted

Cody more than anyone else, except his father, but his actions over the years told a different story. After a long conversation, Lance promised Cody more responsibility and less oversight. His friend and foreman had thrived.

And Lance had floundered.

With almost nothing to do at work because of the permit issues, missing Daisy had consumed him. His dad and Marianne were still dating, spending nearly every evening together. Lance was happy for his dad, but hanging out with his dad and his girlfriend didn't exactly make him feel better about his own dating situation.

In the weeks since his permit issues had mysteriously gone away, Lance had spent every spare minute catching up on the various jobsites and laying the groundwork to make sure something like that never happened again. It had been an entire month of long hours and emergency business first aid.

Lance was determined to get his tools from Daisy today. He hadn't called her, but he'd prayed she would be there. Another step of faith. If they were meant to talk today, she would be there. If he should just let it be, he'd grab his tools and go, and look for another opportunity. God would open the door to their relationship if it was meant to be. Daisy hadn't responded to his texts at Christmas. He didn't know what that meant.

A grin spread across his face when Lance opened his truck door and heard the familiar sound of Daisy's 80s ballads playing loudly inside the house. Lance marveled at her resilience. He'd been tempted to give up in the face of the challenges from the county, and they seemed microscopic compared to the opposition Daisy faced. Not only did she have the inspector, but she had the mystery bullies online. Yet, here she was. Working.

Lance knocked on the door before stepping inside, knowing she wouldn't hear it, but feeling he didn't have the freedom to walk in. This wasn't his jobsite anymore, and that was his own fault. He glanced around the space, amazed at the transformation. The dining room table was set with dishes and centerpieces and napkins. It looked like a spread from a magazine.

To his left, the parlor flowed into the rear living room with more couches and chairs. Bookshelves against the wall housed knickknacks, and plants were scattered between books. The room was homey and inviting, and Lance wanted to sit down and take a nap with the impossibly soft blanket his fingertips traced on the back of the loveseat.

A statue on an end table caught his eye, and he crossed to it, studying the gleaming metallic form. The dancer seemed to float in her dress, arms extended over head in graceful lines.

The memory of Daisy dancing in the empty bedroom upstairs, her toes leaving trails in the sawdust, assaulted him. His fingertips extended toward the statue, desperate to find out if the metal finish was playing tricks on him, because the dancer looked impossibly soft despite the medium. They moved closer and when barely an inch remained, footsteps sounded behind him and he froze.

Lance turned and swallowed disappointment when it wasn't Daisy. Lavender was carrying a large digital camera and a small black shoulder bag. Daisy wore hers tied back in a simply ponytail, Lavender's lighter hair cascaded over her shoulders.

Lavender stopped on the bottom stair, watching him with a guarded expression. The music still played loudly from the speakers they'd installed throughout the house. Lavender waved him outside where she finally spoke to him, her words coming with clouds of warmth in the icy winter air.

"Why are you here, Lance?"

Not a fantastic start. Where was the 'Hey Lance, good to see you'? But he brushed aside the self-doubt and answered Lavender honestly.

"I'm here to pick up my tools." She raised her eyebrow at him and he continued, "And to see Daisy, hopefully."

Lavender pursed her lips to one side and wrinkled her brow. Before she could tell him off, he jumped in. "Please? I need to see her if she's here. It's important."

Lavender glanced back toward the front door, confirming what he thought. Daisy was here.

"Thanks," he said and started back inside.

Lavender stopped him with one hand on his arm, "Wait."

Lance turned back toward her, curious. He'd never really talked to Lavender. From what Daisy had told him, she was brilliant when it came to things online, but she rarely interacted with anyone outside of her computer screen.

Lavender studied him and nodded. "She blames herself. But that doesn't mean she's not mad at you."

Good to know. Lance patted her hand and let himself back into the house he'd become so familiar with. He took the steps two at a time and turned the corner, following the off-key singing that echoed from the blue bathroom.

Daisy sang while she painted. It was the only job they'd done together where she insisted on a boom box and spent as much time singing as she did working. Painting in the blue bathroom must mean...

Lance stopped in the doorway, looking over the gleaming tiles and new vanity. Not a trace of blue to be found. While he studied the space from baseboard to ceiling fan, the singing stopped, and brought his focus to the centerpiece of the room. Daisy stood on the lid of the toilet tank, trimming the line where the ceiling meets the wall with the relaxing blue-green she'd been so proud to show him.

Lance watched, wide-eyed as Daisy turned sharply toward him and lost her balance. Flecks of paint flew from her paintbrush as she windmilled her arms trying to recover, but lost the battle. She stepped back onto the seat and fell to the floor, dropping the paint brush with a clatter Lance couldn't hear over the music.

He stepped toward her, concerned she might be hurt, but Daisy held up a hand to stop him. She sat on the floor and howled with laughter. Finally, Lance found the remote for the music and punched the mute button, filling the tiny room with blessed silence, except for the slowly quieting sound of Daisy.

Lance tried to help her up, but she waved him off. Her laughter subsided, and she stood, composing herself.

"Something about you makes me lose all my natural grace, Lance Matthews."

"Natural grace, eh? I'll believe it when I see it." Of course, he had seen it. When she danced, it was hard to believe she was the same person who fell through the ceiling on his first visit.

She smiled politely and asked, "Are you here for your tools?"

Lance nodded, "Yes, but I also thought we should talk." Nearly two months had passed since the inspector had stopped everything in its tracks—the construction and the relationship.

Daisy set the paintbrush on a paper towel and wiped her hands on a rag dotted with splashes of the paint. "It's fine, Lance. I understand why you left, and I'm sorry my problems made things difficult for you." Picking at a drop of dried paint on the side of her finger, Daisy refused to meet his eyes. Finally, he could see her face and understand. He'd hurt her by leaving, and thinking a text message or two would fix that was underestimating how much.

"I shouldn't have left. I panicked."

Daisy nodded, "You had a business to take care of, I understand."

Lance shook his head and stepped closer to her, forcing her to meet his gaze. "I should have stayed. Yes, I had a business. But I also had you. And that was more important, even if I didn't realize it at the time."

Color rose in Daisy's cheeks and she stepped back. "You deserve someone who won't drive you crazy with mess. The inspector was just another verification that I was right. We are too different." Lance was having deja vu, back in the crawl space having his heart handed back to him. Was the woman so stubborn?

"You don't think what we had is worth fighting for?"

Daisy opened her arms and looked around the small bathroom. "I have other things to fight for right now. And just because the project is done, I'm not suddenly a different person. I'm still going to misplace receipts and forget my wallet. Can you really deal with that long term?"

Lance smiled weakly, "I'd like the chance to try."

Daisy shrugged. "I'm sorry, Lance. I need to focus on this right now. It's too important. I lost one dream when I hurt my ankle and couldn't dance. Part of my spirit died in that hospital room. I'm afraid being with you would kill the rest of it."

Lance frowned. What did that mean? Noticing his confusion, Daisy continued, "Don't you see, Lance? If we were together, I would want to please you. I would bend over backwards trying to be the woman you want—perfectly hung towels and no trace of dirty dishes in the sink." She shook her head. "Where does that leave me?"

Lance shrugged, still not seeing the big deal. "Enjoying clean dishes and dry towels?"

Daisy smiled. "Maybe. Or maybe it would leave me stressed out and bitter, unable to find my creative release within the confines of the rigid structure you thrive in."

Oh.

Is that what would happen? Lance had never thought of it that way. When he envisioned the future, he saw them sharing dinners and DIY projects. Would he, unknowingly, impose his inflexible expectations on her? Would being with a stick in the mud like him ruin her natural vivacious spirit?

What a travesty that would be. To picture Daisy, wilted and depressed, stuck with him when she would rather be somewhere else—like his mother.

But unlike his mother, Daisy wouldn't leave. She was too loyal, too committed. She would stay. And she would be miserable.

Somehow, that was worse.

Lance tucked his hands in his pockets and ducked his head. "Okay. I won't push you. I'll just grab my tools and leave you to it." He glanced around the room. "Looks good in here, by the way." And it did. Daisy had learned a few things along the way, and Lance surged with pride at her tenacity.

"Thanks." She stepped past him and into the hallway, her vanilla and honey shampoo tickling his nose and sending a dull ache into his chest and throat. "I've got your tools all packed up. They're in the sunroom."

Lance followed Daisy down the stairs, impressed again at how the vision for the house had come together. The piles of supplies had disappeared and even Daisy's old room gave the impression of a hotel, with only a few personal touches. It was a far cry from the giant pile of boxes and laundry he remembered walking past before.

Was it just because Lavender was taking pictures and Daisy was getting ready to rent out rooms? Or was she changing without even realizing it? It was foolish to get his hopes up, but Lance couldn't help the feeling that while this might be goodbye, it didn't mean forever. He had to trust God. If he was meant to be with Daisy, God would work out the timing.

Lance and Daisy each carried a box of tools out to his truck and the tailgate shut with a bang. They stood facing each other, the awkwardness palpable. Five months ago, Daisy had fallen through the ceiling and nearly kicked him in the face. Three months ago, they'd kissed in the crawl space and then agreed not to date. Two months ago, she'd melted into his arms and they'd discovered they were better as a team. And one month ago, their differences had seemed insurmountable as opposition rose against her business, and his by extension.

Lance pulled her in for a hug, grateful when she came willingly—almost as though she needed it as much as he did. He desperately wanted her to be the one, but he needed her to want it too. If she were afraid of losing herself, it would never work. Lance needed to be sure he could give grace over and over, like he had been given. He couldn't be trying to change her.

Lance's cheek rested against the crown of her head, and he inhaled the familiar fragrance of vanilla and honey. Daisy's head was nestled on his shoulder —a perfect fit, as though he were designed solely for this purpose. Slowly, he tipped his chin and softly pressed his lips to the golden tresses, with pressure so slight Daisy might not even notice. Somehow, he had to let go of this woman.

For now.

With one last squeeze, Lance memorized the feel of her body against his. Maybe, in God's time, they would both be ready.

Until then, Lance would remember this hug.

And he would pray.

26

*D*aisy walked back inside after waving one last goodbye to Lance. That was it. His tools were gone and so was he. She perched on the wicker sofa in the sunroom and looked at the now-empty spot where his tools had been. Daisy said what she needed to say, the truth rolling around her head since the day he left. But it didn't make it hurt any less.

If Daisy were with him, she would lose part of herself. And she couldn't do that again. Her dream was enough, and her independence was critical. Her happiness depended on it. Didn't it?

Still, it was hard to see him go. Part of her longed to run back to the porch and chase the white truck down the gravel road, begging him to come back.

The memories of being together called to her. Flirting while hanging cabinets. Long drives in his truck. Kissing in the kitchen. Instead, Daisy retreated up the stairs to finish the bathroom.

Everyone in her family came to see the house the other day, and they'd all ooohed and aaahhhed in the right places, amazed at the changes she'd made in the last six months. But none of their compliments had meant as much as Lance's simple comment about the bathroom she'd done without him.

Daisy had finally earned the approval of the nitpicky slave driver she paid for months to teach her and work alongside her. Every contractor who had laughed or leered at her? They could eat dirt.

The bed-and-breakfast opened in a month, just in time for beautiful romantic spring getaways. Lavender took pictures this morning of everything except the blue bathroom. Daisy would probably always think of it that way. It wasn't actually blue anymore, but the legacy would live on in conversation long after the dumpster with blue tiles and countertop was hauled away.

Daisy had proven she could do anything she set her mind to. Well, with God's help. Because even though He hadn't picked up a screwdriver, God had been with her. When doubts came, she felt Him reassuring her. When she forgot something, the memory of a video would come to mind. There was no doubt God was showing her that He would see her through.

Daisy had to believe everything would work out. God had a plan in all of this. Still, the doubts lingered. What if she opened the B&B for reservations and the calendar stayed completely empty? All her hard work would be for naught. Sure, this house was beautiful now. She glanced around the inviting, cozy space. It was ready to be filled with laughter and love. For nearly thirty years, it sat empty on the property. Now, the historic home was ready to show off for the world.

As long as people came.

Four weeks later, the sponsored ad on Lance's social media feed stared back at him. The familiar staircase and gleaming hardwood floors mocked him. The comfortable and airy seating area he remembered from his last visit to Bloom's Farm called to him from the background. Go back, it said.

Lance clicked on the advertisement, unable to resist. The website was fresh, professional, and full of impressive photos on a slideshow. A video prompt invited him to press play. Behind the triangle icon, he saw the familiar silhouette of Daisy.

Hesitantly, he tapped the mouse and soft music overlaid with Daisy's familiar lilting voice greeted him through the speakers. A lonely ache clenched his heart and he closed his eyes. How could he miss her this much? Even the sound of her voice was overwhelming. Lance forced his eyes open and watched as Daisy pointed out the features of Bloom's Farm B&B as she took him on a tour.

Instead of looking at the rooms, Lance studied her face. At first glance, she seemed relaxed and confident. To anyone else, she would be the perfect vision of a successful business owner, inviting them to come and stay. But Lance wasn't just anyone. There was strain around her eyes, despite the makeup he'd never seen her wear before. She pulled her hair over one shoulder, as though tempted to pull it into a ponytail instead of the soft, straight, golden waterfall.

Daisy looked happy. But were those circles under her eyes, or just shadows? Was Lance imagining problems where there were none? What about the fake reviews?

Lance found the search bar and typed in Bloom's

Farm Bed and Breakfast. Five stars. No matter which review site he clicked on, he couldn't find any trace of the negative reviews claiming that patrons would get food poisoning.

He didn't know how Daisy or Lavender had done it, but they had. Lance shouldn't have doubted. Daisy would go after her dreams with everything she had. Her methods might be different from his, but God had given Daisy a call and she was being obedient. That was admirable.

Lance was doing his best to do the same, to be obedient and surrender his own tight grip of control. Trusting God didn't come easy to a man who worked tireless to ensure his own desired outcomes—stability and financial success.

Was it time to follow up with Daisy again? He prayed about it, trying to listen, unsure if the surge of hope was a sign from God or just his own desires screaming at him to pursue the woman he loved.

He loved Daisy.

It shouldn't come as a surprise, but it did. When they were together—even before they were together —he would do anything for her. His days were better when he saw her, even when she did things that irritated him. Lance wanted to be the one she leaned on after the hard days and celebrated with on the good days. He wanted to dance with her, despite his own clumsy feet.

Agreeing to work on the house had started with a promise to his father and turned to professional interest at the sight of the historic property. When he discovered the heart of the project—Daisy—it had become so much more.

Getting to know Daisy, and falling for her, had turned a simple side project into something important. Lance was personally invested, not because he wanted to see the project completed, but because he needed to see Daisy achieve her dream.

Now, he needed to see it in person. With one last prayer that his timing was right, he clicked the Reserve Now button. Then he grabbed his notebook and started a new to-do list, perhaps the most important one he would ever write.

27

*D*aisy and Lavender huddled over the computer tucked in the corner of the parlor. The gorgeous antique secretary desk would act as the check-in desk for the B&B, and the grand opening was only a week away. Whatever Lavender had been doing with advertising was apparently working, because opening weekend was already fully booked, and Daisy was thrilled to see no familiar names. Actual strangers found her business and decided to stay there!

This week, Jacquie and Roger, along with her friend Mandy and her new husband, Garrett, would spend the night at the bed-and-breakfast as a dry-run. Jacquie breezed through the front door, her shiny black leather handbag on her elbow and her sparkly black sheath trailing behind her. Daisy looked up from the desk and grinned at the familiar face of her mentor and godmother.

"Daisy!" Jacquie spun around, "The place looks fabulous!" Daisy crossed the distance and pulled Jacquie into a hug.

"I'm so glad you are here," she said and turned to Roger. "Thank you so much for coming!"

"Of course! We wouldn't miss the chance to see our goddaughter embark on such an exciting venture."

Daisy blushed, "I wouldn't be here without your help." Without Jacquie's encouragement and generosity, the bed-and-breakfast would still be an empty shell of a house. That, or Daisy would be knee-deep in a bitter online feud with the Butterfly Inn. But Jacquie had been right. God called Daisy and protected her. When the time had finally come to address the unwarranted attacks, He'd been there and given her the patience and words to diffuse the situation. What could have been the start of a long feud was resolved with a simple conversation. Mr. Havershem's sister agreed to remove all the fake reviews and Daisy agreed to refer business to the Butterfly Inn if the B&B was overbooked.

The final months of the project—her dad's

stroke, the reviews, and the inspector—God had seen her through it, even when she hadn't been aware of it. Having to say goodbye to Lance? It was one more thing Daisy had done she wasn't sure she could.

Not a day went by that she hadn't thought about him. When she'd finally finished the blue bathroom, she'd wanted to show him. When the first real reservation came through the website, the first person she wanted to celebrate with was Lance. Instead, she'd sent Andi an email with far too many exclamation points and gone to find her parents. But the longing to feel him hug and spin her around with a laugh hadn't gone away.

Perhaps the strangest part was realizing that she was changing. Hawthorne had been the first one to point out that she'd stopped leaving empty Diet Dr. Pepper cans around. She'd frowned at him, her hand hovering over the trash can, actually tempted to pull it back out and set it on the counter just to prove she wasn't different.

But the fact was her time with Lance had left some sort of indelible mark on her. It manifested in Daisy keeping the kitchen counters empty and a daily to-do list in block letters not quite as neat as his.

Since the renovation projects ended, Daisy started tackling small furniture makeovers. Daisy found it strangely freeing to add a creative project into the carefully planned schedule. Was there such a thing as structured creativity?

She'd always assumed if she tried to contain her creative spark, the flame would wither altogether. Yet, within the small confines of the shed behind the bed-and-breakfast, Daisy was free to paint a dresser teal and the handles pink. Better yet, she was free to leave the mess, or clean it up—depending on her mood.

It was just another thing she wanted to share with Lance. When she went shopping for a hand-held sander, Daisy nearly called for his opinion. When she wasn't quite sure how to reinforce a broken drawer on a nightstand, she had snapped a picture and was halfway through texting him before second-guessing herself.

When she hit his name to send the picture, their previous conversations had popped up and stopped her in her tracks. A few awkward messages from Christmas Day she never responded to. Above that, her message telling him not to come back after Larry Havershem had dropped the bombshell of suspended permits on them both. And above that? One from him from that morning.

Good morning, Beautiful. I'll be there in 20 minutes.

Had she made a mistake? Was it possible for people so different to love each other? Lance had said he wanted the chance to put up with her every day. But could she do the same?

The idea of trying again had been swirling around endlessly, but today she needed to push it away. She had guests to take care of, and right now, there was nothing more important. Daisy gave Jacquie and Roger a tour of the property, talking about the changes she had made and the pieces of the original house that remained.

Daisy showed them to their room, her eyes instinctively finding the unnoticeable place where the ceiling had been patched after her first encounter with Lance. Would every corner of this house always remind her of him?

After leaving her first guests to get settled, she walked back downstairs. Her chef hadn't started yet, but Poppy had whipped up a few small appetizers for an evening reception and she knew most of her siblings, plus Avery, would be coming by to celebrate with her. Her mom was confident Dad would be there, too, which was a testament to how much he had recovered in just three months.

Hawthorne would officially move out this week, back into the main house—at least for a while. Daisy had a feeling it wouldn't be long before Storybook Barn would host its first Bloom Family wedding. Hawthorne was absolutely head over heels for Avery, and by this time next year, she would have to add another sister to the already long list.

Next weekend, the guests would be strangers and a party would be out of place, but tonight Daisy was determined to enjoy every second. Even if there was one notable absence from the celebration.

Mandy and Garrett checked in an hour later, and when five o'clock rolled around, hungry siblings started wandering in—Hawthorne first, of course. He leaned in and gave her a hug.

"Congratulations, Daze. You really did it."

Daisy smiled, "Thanks." She didn't do it alone, though. Lance should be here.

Avery knocked lightly on the doorframe as she opened the door and peeked around, before her eyes widened at the space. "Daisy! This looks amazing!" Her friend gave her a quick squeeze before claiming her place at Hawthorne's side, where she would likely remain for most of the evening.

Lavender came through the back door, camera in hand. She held it up to Daisy and gestured to the dining room, "I'm going to grab some pictures with the food on display. Placeholders for the catering website." Then she ducked out of sight.

Jacquie and Roger came downstairs and greeted Hawthorne who introduced them to Avery with a proud smile. Hawthorne's transformation was nothing less than a miracle in Daisy's mind. Sometimes it was still surprising to see him embracing the responsibility and commitment of a relationship, and his new role on the farm as General Manager.

Lily and Poppy came in together, followed shortly after by Rose, helping Mom support their dad as he struggled up the porch stairs. Her dad's determination was evident in his gritted teeth. Daisy waited patiently inside the door for him. It was hard to watch her father struggle and not jump in to help. No doubt each of her siblings felt the same. Hawthorne watched, poised to intervene at the slightest sign of wavering.

Keith sighed heavily as he reached the top step and then shuffled slowly across the porch to the door. Daisy grinned broadly and embraced his surprisingly soft frame. Maybe now she was seeing where she got her tenacity.

He spoke softly into her ear, "Pro...Prow-duh."

Proud. Tears stung the back of Daisy's eyes, and the lump rose in her throat.

"Me too," she whispered before releasing him.

Everyone shuffled around, making space for her dad to navigate to the living room and sit in an armchair. Jacquie and Roger sat close, talking with their longtime friends.

Daisy watched as Rose efficiently gathered everything her father might need. Water with a straw appeared on the side table, plus a small plate with appetizers and extra napkins, since he still had some trouble swallowing.

Rose, out of all of them, was closest to their father. She loved the animals the same way he always had. Being the youngest, she'd always had a special place on their father's lap when driving the tractor or riding a horse, until she'd been old enough to do all those things on her own.

Daisy wrapped an arm around her youngest sister and gave her a squeeze, laying her cheek on her sister's dark hair. "How are you doing, Rose?"

Rose answered without removing her eyes from their father. "I'm okay. I've been better, but it's going to be alright." Finally, Rose looked up at Daisy. "I can't believe this place is really done."

Daisy laughed, "I know. I thought it would never happen."

Rose nodded sadly, "I know what you mean."

Wrinkles creased Daisy's forehead. Before Daisy could question her further, Rose ducked out of her embrace with a casual line about getting herself a drink.

Daisy saw Mandy and Garrett chatting with Lily. Mandy's wedding was held at Storybook Barn back in October. It seemed like five years instead of five months ago. That night, Daisy had been the Maid of Honor, dancing with Mandy's brother, Josh, and convincing herself she didn't wish it was Lance.

Tonight, Daisy was the center of attention, which she'd always loved. More so when she was dancing and all eyes were on her, but this was sort of the same—a performance. It was the unveiling of the hard work she'd done over the last year. Like finally showing the world after months and months of rehearsal.

At the same time, tonight was ultimately the dress rehearsal for next weekend and every night after where strangers and guests would fill this house. Still, she couldn't help but wish there was a different set of eyes watching the show tonight.

28

*L*ance packed his small duffel bag. He had two days to convince her they were right for each other and that he could coexist with her "creative spirit." Which was another word for disorganized mess, but he was trying to reframe his attitude.

Waves of heat washed over him and his hands started to sweat. Lance wiped the clammy skin on his jeans and sent a quick prayer heavenward. This had to work. Visions of the gorgeous oak door being slammed in his face brought his eyes open wide in an instant.

Check in started at 3 pm. He pulled into the gravel parking area at 3:15, pleased to see no other cars there. He had Daisy all to himself for at least a minute.

When he made the reservation a month ago, it was impulsive. Temporary insanity, right? Wasn't that a legal defense? He'd considered canceling it a dozen times. Even pulled up the confirmation email and clicked the button. But when the pop-up questioned him—accused him, really—are you sure you want to cancel? He'd been unable to do it.

Canceling would be admitting that he and Daisy were done. So, instead, he'd continued to pray. Lance knew changing Daisy was the wrong goal. So, he tested himself, leaving dirty laundry on the floor next to the hamper instead of putting it where it belonged. Two days passed before he needed to move it, which he thought was pretty good. He left his mail unfiled in a stack on the counter and left the bed unmade. It hadn't come naturally, but it hadn't made him crazy either.

Lance was ready. Anticipation had been slowly building, along with the anxiety, for weeks. Tonight was the night. His reservation was under the name Matthew Chance. As in, please give Matthews a chance. Had she noticed?

Would she suspect it was him?

When Hawthorne stepped out on the porch,

Lance felt the breath catch in his throat. Daisy knew, and she'd pulled in her brother to tell him off! Lance didn't move a muscle as Hawthorne jogged down the steps and gave a nonchalant wave. His step faltered and he backtracked, changing his path to walk up to Lance's truck. Lance rolled down the window, unwilling to step outside, just in case Hawthorne was the type to throw a punch.

A genuine smile greeted him though, and Lance relaxed when Hawthorne spoke. "Lance! Good to see you, man. I didn't know you were coming by." A worried frown flickered. "Didn't you and Daisy..."

Lance quirked an eyebrow. "Break up? Yeah."

"Okay, so why are you here?"

Lance sighed and stared at the steering wheel as he mumbled, "Because I love her."

The impact of Hawthorne's gloved hands on the window frame made Lance jump. Gleaming white teeth flashed with Hawthorne's smile, "Hallelujah!"

At Lance's questioning look, Hawthorne continued. "At least one of you has some sense. Daisy's been puttering around like a stray sheep, trying so hard to convince herself she's happy that she can't admit she's lost."

Lance's heart skipped. "Really?"

Hawthorne nodded, looked toward the house and back at Lance. "She know you're coming?"

Lance shook his head, "It's a surprise."

Hawthorne chuckled, "Well, that ought to be interesting. Wish I could stick around for the fireworks, but I need to run down to see Rose."

They said goodbye, Hawthorne wished him luck, and Lance took a deep breath.

More confidently than his racing heart would suggest, he grabbed his small duffel bag from the passenger seat and stepped out of the truck. This has to work, God.

DAISY FUSSED with the flowers on the dining table, freshly picked this morning from the flower shop in Minden. Making last minute adjustments was the only thing she could think to do. Guests could arrive any minute.

Of course, they might not arrive until ten o'clock tonight. That was one downside of running the bed-and-breakfast. She needed to find something she could do during the downtime. Preferably something that didn't involve spray paint or smelling like varnish, as she so often did during her days off, spent on projects in the shed.

Daisy pulled a carnation to the front, leaned back to study it and then shifted it back where it was. The faint thud of a car door caught her attention and she glanced toward the front door. Were they here? Would it be Mr. and Mrs. Higgins? Or maybe the Porter family? Or Matthew Chance? The name sounded so familiar, but she couldn't place it.

Maybe he would be cute and take her mind off Lance.

A knock sounded at the door and she hurried to it, leaving her obsessive flower fidgeting behind.

Daisy grabbed the door with a broad smile and opened her arm to welcome her first guest inside the foyer. "Welcome to Bloo—" she stopped mid word, the sound dying on her lips and her wide smile dropping open in a gasp. Her heart was in her throat, beating rapidly, screaming at her to step toward him.

He couldn't be here, she had guests coming. Lance couldn't be here! How dare he show up to ruin her grand opening.

Then Daisy spotted the overnight bag in his left hand.

Her mind flew through the options. Lance

Matthews. Matthew Chance. Sneaky sneaky, Mr. Matthews.

How should she handle this? Slamming the door seemed like a safe option. But technically, he'd done nothing wrong. They'd parted two months ago with a hug. Maybe not as friends, but not as people who would refuse to talk.

Daisy sighed and tipped her head toward the living room. Might as well have this out now. Closing the door behind him, she gestured him toward the couch.

She took the chair next to his, closing her eyes when the storm clouds in his own called out. "Lance, you—"

"I've got a reservation."

She opened her eyes, "Lance," she pleaded.

"I'd like to check in, please," he said stubbornly.

Daisy sighed. He didn't want to talk?

"Name?"

"Lance Matthews."

She pressed her lips together and shook her head. "I'm sorry sir, I don't have a reservation by that name." He wasn't the only one who could play this game.

"Hmm, I must have made a typo. Let me find my confirmation." He rummaged through the pockets in his bag. "I know I've got it here somewhere."

What was he doing? Lance had never misplaced anything in his life. Finally, he pulled a rumpled paper from a side pocket and smoothed it out. "Oh, would you look at that. I accidentally made the reservation for Matthew Chance." His wide eyes twinkled as he handed her the paper. "That won't be a problem, will it, Miss Bloom? You are Miss Bloom, I assume?" he asked with wide, innocent eyes.

His acting skills were terrible, and the smile teased at her lips. Daisy bit it back and cleared her throat. He wasn't going to make this easy. Daisy should make him leave—refuse to play along with whatever this little charade was. But she felt lighter than she had in weeks, and she wanted to see where it went.

She could still say goodbye to him at the end of the weekend. They were friends, right? It would be nice to have a familiar face at the inn this weekend. Slowly, she talked herself into letting him stay.

"That will be just fine, Mr. Matthews. Let me get you checked in on the computer here, and I'll show you up to your room."

Lance flashed a broad smile, the joy of victory painted on his face as she stood. Daisy wavered, the inevitable off-balance feeling that came from proximity to Lance was back. She reached down to catch herself on the arm of the chair, but Lance was there. He caught her hand and shoulder, steadying her. Her skin burned where he touched her, as though his touch carried the memories of their kisses.

She glanced up at him, and saw his dark eyes glued to hers.

"Daisy, I—" he whispered, his voice strangled and rough.

The need in his voice almost brought Daisy to her knees, and she jerked away, taking a roundabout path around the furniture to avoid being close to him. Daisy cleared her throat and blinked after turning her face away, as though she could reset her internal awareness of him and start over.

"I'll just need your credit card, Mr. Matthews." Intentionally, she filled her voice with polite professionalism. His jaw tightened, and he nodded.

"Sure. I'll just have to find my wallet," with the words, Lance winked at her and heat rose in her cheeks. "I'm sure it is in here somewhere."

Something about his mischievous grin told her this was going to be a very long weekend.

29

*S*afely ensconced in the same room where Daisy had fallen through the ceiling and nearly kicked him in the nose, Lance had to wonder if she'd chosen it on purpose. He laid on the bed, remarkably comfortable, and slipped off his shoes, leaving them on the rug. He would probably trip over them later.

If this weekend was going to work, he had to be fully committed. Lance hadn't expected Daisy to fall into his arms when he showed up on her porch. It would have been nice, though. At least she hadn't kicked him out. Lance had an entire weekend to convince Daisy he was the only one for her.

Even if she was practically tripping over her own feet to put some distance between them. It wasn't the first time she'd run away instead of facing her feelings. Kissing him in the crawlspace was the first of many times where Daisy admitted feelings for him and then talked herself out of them.

This weekend, he needed to quell those objections. It shouldn't be hard. They were the same misgivings he'd wrestled with. The two of them were different—wildly different. When it came to tackling a problem, he and Daisy had radically different approaches. When it came to cleanliness, Lance was 'socks arranged by color' and she was 'socks that might or might not match'. But they shared important things too.

Faith.

Loyalty to family.

A love of restoration.

Irresistible chemistry.

With important things like that unifying them, the rest seemed terribly unimportant. When he admired her sense of adventure, her confidence and her vivacious spirit; it seemed foolish to dismiss a future because she sometimes forgot to turn off the lights.

He just had to convince her of the same thing. Starting today.

Lance flipped through the welcome packet,

which highlighted the amenities of the bed-and-breakfast and nearby attractions. Along with local state parks, restaurants, wineries, and the tourist-centered dairy farm an hour away, Bloom's Farm invited the guests of the bed-and-breakfast to explore the farm on horseback, visit and taste the offerings of Poppy's winery, or bottle-feed baby goats. He skimmed the note page, making note of one sentence in particular: To arrange farm excursions, contact Daisy Bloom or the host for your stay.

An idea began to spark, and Lance smiled to himself. He knew Daisy wouldn't want to leave this evening, at least not until after all the guest were checked in. But tomorrow? He was going to shamelessly guilt her into spending the day with him.

He grabbed a book from his bag and made his way downstairs again. Daisy might hope he would stay in his room all weekend, but he had other plans. Starting with seeing Daisy as much as possible.

Daisy ran the feather duster over the already clean shelves, stealing glances at the man who seemed to dominate the space in the parlor. Lance looked far too comfortable in the cozy room, casually reading a book. She tried to peer around a lamp to read the title on the cover, extending to her tiptoes and leaning over to one side. Lance hadn't even looked up from the book since he sat down, despite her flitting around the room.

Daisy wasn't exactly trying to get his attention, but wasn't he there for a reason? What book could possibly have him so enraptured? Lance shifted his weight and Daisy startled, her back foot coming off the ground, the feather duster flailing through the air as she tried to catch her balance. Why did this always happen around him? She had been a professional dancer, for crying out loud!

She caught herself, her foot coming down loudly on the wood floor. Daisy winced and opened one eye to see if Lance had reacted.

He flipped a page, and she narrowed her eyes. He was doing this on purpose, right? Ignoring her?

Should she say something?

Daisy walked around in front of him and fluffed the pillows, already perfectly staged. Finally, she caught a glimpse of the cover of the book that had him so entranced. *Who Moved My Cheese?*

A snort escaped before she could stop it, and she covered her mouth. Piercing brown eyes shifted up toward her, his expression teasing, even as his words betrayed nothing. "Have you read this book?" He held up the cover so she could see it clearly.

Daisy pressed her lips together and shook her head. "Not exactly something I struggle with."

Lance nodded and placed a finger on his chin as though she'd said the most philosophical thing in history and he needed time to properly digest the wisdom.

"You know," he said after a long pause, "I've been told I'm too rigid."

"You don't say?" Daisy couldn't help but respond sarcastically, hearing him quote her own words about him.

Lance nodded. "I know, hard to believe, isn't it?" A chuckle escaped from Daisy and he continued, "But, I'm learning that perhaps my way isn't always the best way."

"Thus, the book?" she replied skeptically. It was one thing to say the right words, or even to read the right book. But what about the reality?

"Yes, the book. And other things."

"Oh?"

"I'm finding that the more I surround myself with people who operate with more flexibility—the more my own way of thinking changes."

Daisy couldn't respond. A faint glimmer of hope

flickered inside her, and she desperately tried to squash it.

"For example, there was this woman." Daisy raised her eyebrows. "She taught me a lot about the... merits of creative thinking."

Daisy needed an escape and looked around desperately for a way out, but Lance kept talking. "The more time we spent together, the more I wanted—"

The knock on the door interrupted him, and Daisy's heart clamored at the intrusion. What did Lance want more of?

Lance disappeared while she checked in the Porter family. While she was charmed by the nine- and eleven-year-old brothers and their friendly parents, Daisy hadn't appreciated the interruption and wanted to continue the conversation.

Daisy thought she would be happy for him to get out of her sight. He'd been lounging around like he owned the place since he checked in, and her awareness of Lance's presence was making it impossible to concentrate. Not that there was much to concentrate on. Everything had been ready for days. Washing sheets and cleaning up after the previous weekend had taken up her Monday, but beyond that? She'd been pacing and trying not to be anxious about the grand opening. Daisy needed everything to go well, if only to prove to herself that it could.

She knew there would be hiccups along the way, and that sometimes guests would cancel or complain. But the first real weekend needed to be a success.

And then Lance shows up on her front step and derails the whole thing. What was he thinking? Daisy needed to remember why she and Lance hadn't worked in the first place. He had walked out, frustrated and blaming her for shutting down his business. Which had been her fault. Getting involved again would only lead to trouble for both of them.

Clearly, Lance had forgotten. It was up to her to remember for both of them. She didn't have time for philosophical discussions about how Lance thought his rigidity and her carefree attitude could coexist.

When she'd walked past his room to take the Porter family to their rooms, she spotted his open suitcase on the bed and a dirty pair of socks on the rug. It seemed uncharacteristic of him, to say the least. But she'd never been to his house. Maybe he was a slob.

Even as she had the thought, she laughed at it. Lance could be called many things—inflexible, demanding, intense, driven, thoughtful, handsome...

She shook away the list of increasingly positive attributes. Lance was many things, but slob was not on the list.

After the Porters checked in, Daisy gave them directions to Minden so they could grab dinner at B&J Bistro and enjoy the small-town shops. Dinner sounded good, but her final guests hadn't arrived, and she needed to stick around. The gourmet kitchen was perhaps her favorite room in the inn, even though she didn't cook herself. It had been a key point of her vision, and she'd made it happen. Whenever she pulled a dish from the cupboard, she knew she had driven in the screws holding it up.

There was one thing missing from the kitchen, though.

Food.

Oh, there were plenty of ingredients—supplies her chef, Bonnie, would use tomorrow morning to make apple-cinnamon French toast and eggs to order. Nothing for dinner, though. Daisy grabbed a Diet Dr. Pepper from the bottom shelf of the fridge and popped it open. At least she had the essentials. Dinner would have to wait until later. Surely her mom or Lily had something she could grab after all the guests were settled in.

A car door slammed, and she ventured to the

window, hopeful the Higgins were here, but Lance was jogging up the steps holding a plastic bag with a familiar logo. He stepped inside and wiped his shoes carefully on the welcome mat. She waited as he walked through the parlor and around the living room. He continued toward the kitchen and finally spotted her watching him. Daisy hid her smile behind her soda can, unwilling to show her reaction to his presence.

Lance held up the bag, "Somewhere I can eat this?"

Silently answering, Daisy gestured to the dining room. Then, determined to be a good hostess, she pulled a plate and silverware from the kitchen and brought them to him.

"Thank you! I'm starving." He pulled a takeout container from the bag and the scent of garlic wafted toward her, sparking the hunger she'd tried to quiet with soda. Lance continued speaking casually, "I think I accidentally ordered too much food. Would you care to join me?"

Daisy smirked. He was too obvious and totally shameless! Sure, he just happened to accidentally order two full entrees at the bistro?

Still, when he opened the boxes, she couldn't help but look at the Friday night pasta special with longing. Her mouth watered, and she swallowed heavily.

Lance looked up at her hopefully, still trying to maintain his nonchalance.

"I really shouldn't."

"Come on, it's just dinner."

It wasn't just dinner, though. It was an invitation to so much more, and Daisy was desperately afraid saying yes to takeout would lead to saying yes to other things. Although, an increasingly large part of her was screaming that saying yes wouldn't be so bad.

Lance must have sensed her resistance softening and dished up a portion onto the plate she'd brought him. He slid it in front of the chair she stood behind.

He stepped through the French doors into the kitchen, and she heard opening cabinets and drawers while she studied the plate of food. Lance came back carrying a second plate and silverware, plus napkins and glasses.

Hunger won, and she sat, though she couldn't have said whether it was hunger for food or the desire for connection. Lance did an admirable job of concealing his celebratory reaction.

During dinner, Daisy noticed something odd about Lance. He was, personality-wise, the same as he had always been—kind, witty, a good listener. But she noticed other things. Instead of setting his glass on a placemat, it was always on the table. From anyone else, she would not have batted an eye. But for Lance, who had lectured her about coasters and the potential for water rings from her soda cans more than once, it was strange.

When he dripped red pasta sauce on his shirt, an oddity in itself, his reaction was even more striking. Daisy had immediately started to get out of her chair to find him a spot remover or club soda. But Lance? He barely dabbed at the red stain with a napkin before shrugging his shoulders and giving her another of those blasted winks. Who was this and what had happened to Lance Matthews?

30

On Saturday morning, Lance woke early to the smell of coffee and bacon. It was definitely something he could get used to. Last night at dinner, Daisy had shared her excitement about the cook she'd hired—a grandmotherly figure whose years in the kitchen rivaled any professional training.

Today was the day Lance would lay it on the line. He had another night booked at the bed-and-breakfast, but watching Daisy over takeout containers under the dimmed lights in the dining room, he knew he wouldn't make it that long.

If his hunch was right, she was softening. Before anything else, Lance said a variation of the same prayer he'd been praying since he made the reservation. If we aren't supposed to be together, help me accept it. If we are, help me convince Daisy.

Lance got ready and went downstairs. Daisy was waiting in the living room with her ever-present soda can in hand. She greeted him without making eye contact and directed him to choose whichever seat he'd prefer. A short, pillowy woman with white hair and leathery wrinkles bustled through the kitchen doors carrying a basket lined with fabric. She smiled at Lance, and he couldn't help but return the friendly greeting.

"Lance, this is Bonnie. Bonnie, this is Lance Matthews. He was my contractor for most of the project on this house."

Bonnie's eyes lit up, and she welcomed him warmly, offering him the still-warm mini-muffins, "To tide you over until your French toast is ready."

Daisy watched the friendly exchange and interrupted with a teasing tone, "Just be careful, Bonnie. Before you adopt him, you should know he didn't think you needed such an outstanding kitchen."

Bonnie waved a hand, then wagged a finger at her employer. "I don't need such a fancy kitchen, Miss Daisy. For thirty years, I cooked three meals a day for a family of ten in a kitchen half this size!"

Daisy opened her arms in mock disbelief, "Aren't I paying you to be on my side, Bonnie?"

Lance laughed at the expression Bonnie gave him before disappearing back into the kitchen, hollering over her shoulder. "Sorry, dearie. You only pay me to cook!"

Finally meeting Daisy's eyes, Lance watched hers carefully, trying to gauge her mood this morning. Was she already regretting their intimate dinner?

"Good morning, beautiful."

The most delicious shade of rosy pink colored her cheeks, and she hid behind her soda, "Hi."

"Bonnie seems wonderful," he commented. Then, biting into one of the muffins, Lance gave a hum of approval, "And she's definitely got the goods as far as I can tell."

Daisy smiled as she replied, "Doesn't she? It was totally a God thing she was even looking for something to fill her time now that her kids are grown."

Lance had been around Daisy for less than twenty hours, but he'd do whatever it took to convince her to let him stay. There was something about seeing her smile across the room, or hearing her speak so casually about God working in her life. Being back in her orbit was like coming home.

"Daisy, we need—"

Thunderous footsteps down the wooden staircase interrupted him, and seconds later, flashes of color burst through the opening to the hallway into the dining room. The Porter brothers. The boys both tried to claim the chair at the head of the table, attempting to shove and pull each other off.

A shrill whistle cut through the room and Lance winced. "Boys! Enough. Sit." The loud, authoritative voice froze the boys in the middle of the rough-housing. Their father entered the room and conveyed an entire paragraph of instructions to his children with only his eyes and an index finger with impeccable aim. While Daisy greeted the energetic boys and offered them hot cocoa and muffins, Mr. Porter took the chair the boys had been fighting over.

Mrs. Porter followed a minute or two later, a floral cotton robe wrapped over her pajamas.

"Good morning," she yawned. "Coffee?"

Daisy pointed her to the coffee pot set up on the sideboard, neatly arranged with mugs and everything anyone could want in their coffee, tea, or hot chocolate. Daisy had certainly anticipated everything. Pride swelled at the woman standing across the room from him. This was her element, and he felt privileged to experience it. "Help yourself, or take a seat and I'll be happy to bring it to you," Daisy said cheerfully.

Bonnie pushed through the French doors once again with a bright smile. "Good morning, friends! I'm Bonnie Mae and I am so pleased to cook for you this morning." After verifying food allergies and taking orders for eggs, Bonnie disappeared into the kitchen once more.

Mr. and Mrs. Higgins came down twenty minutes into breakfast, after Lance had devoured three slices of apple-cinnamon French toast. The elderly couple ambled across the room. Lance watched, trying not to be too obvious, as Mr. Higgins gently helped his wife into the chair before locating the coffee and fixing his wife a mug.

He brought it to her before returning to the sideboard to get his own cup and take the chair beside her. Conversation flowed amongst the guests, never a dull moment as the Porter boys chattered through any silence, talking about their plans to go hiking today. Though Lance nodded and asked them questions about their adventures, his attention lingered on the tenderness of the couple at the other end of the table.

He watched as Mr. Higgins retrieved his wife's napkin from the floor not once, but three times, and repeated himself several times so she could hear him. There was a powerful tug at his heart when Mrs. Higgins laid her weathered and pale hand on top of her husbands and squeezed gently.

Curiosity niggled and he finally asked, "Mr. Higgins, how long have you been married?"

The old man laughed and patted his wife's hand. "Oh, it's going on sixty years now."

Wow. When Lance congratulated them, Mr. Higgins smiled warmly. "It's not easy. But it's worth it."

THOUGH SHE'D BEEN RUNNING BACK and forth delivering plates for Bonnie and refilling beverages, Daisy watched the exchange between Mr. Higgins and Lance with interest. Apparently, Lance had noticed the same things she had. The love between the two aged souls was so thick it was palpable. Sixty years?

But it was Mr. Higgins last words, simple as they were, that echoed in her mind. It's not easy. But it's worth it. Daisy leaned back against the wall and listened as he continued. "You have someone special, son? Someone you love?"

Lance glanced up at her for a split second, and heat rose in her cheeks again. Then, in an instant, his eyes were back on Mr. Higgins, with a glimmer hidden in their depths. "Well, sir. I'm afraid it's a little complicated at the moment. But I do love her." The serious tone of Lance's voice and the words he'd uttered made Daisy's breath seize in her chest. She stood up straight in surprise. Did Lance actually just declare his love for her to an old man at the breakfast table?

Mr. Higgins gave a toothy grin and glanced at Daisy. "Well, that certainly makes things more interesting around here." He looked back at Lance and spoke again. "Let me give you both some free advice." Daisy heard his words, but her eyes were on Lance, whose gaze was fixed on her. Lance's brown eyes darted to Mr. Higgins, and he nodded, before looking back at her. Her heart fluttered.

"Don't let small things get in the way of what could be the biggest thing. The best thing." Daisy shifted her gaze to the old man as he gently patted his wife's cheek, his voice full of emotion. "And once you decide to love someone, you just make that same decision every day after that, until it is unimaginable to do anything else."

Daisy's heart lurched. Is that how Lance loved

her? Enough to choose it every day for sixty years? Could he love her enough to choose it when she forgot to buy milk or left her clothes on the floor instead of the hamper? And even if he could—could she do it, too? Could she love him when he was driving her crazy with lists or his stubborn refusal to consider another approach?

What if he was the kind of man who got lost and refused to ask for directions? Could she love him even when their differences made her feel unloved or misunderstood?

Unbidden, her eyes locked with Lance's once again. From across the room, his stare burned into her so intensely she thought she might actually burst into flames. Still, this wasn't the right time. The thought was punctuated with the sudden shouts and name-calling erupting from the Porter children. A river of orange juice flowed across the rough-hewn dining table and dripped rapidly to the floor, creating a small puddle that grew with each drop.

Daisy ducked into the kitchen for a towel, returning to sop up the sticky liquid. As she lowered to her knees to wipe the floor, she couldn't help but register the acute absence of Lance from the room. She'd assumed he'd be waiting for her, eager to start

—and finish—the conversation they obviously needed to have.

Lance said he loved her. That couldn't be right, could it? How could an organized, methodical, driven man like Lance love a hot mess like Daisy Bloom? More than anything, she wanted to believe it would work. Sending Lance home tomorrow and never seeing him again would hurt more than any broken ankle. Even the homestead seemed homier when he was in it, like the house itself was convinced it owed Lance Matthews some debt of gratitude for restoring it.

And Daisy? Being around Lance had her unsettled and jittery. Off-balance.

Except when it didn't. Like over dinner when she finally let herself relax and enjoy his company. Or in the moments when she'd fallen into Lance's arms like he could hold her together when she was falling apart, which he had done without reservation.

Loving Lance Matthews would be terrifying. Loving him would be frustrating and exhilarating and wonderful. Admitting to herself what she'd known all along was perhaps the hardest part of all. Loving Lance Matthews was terrifying. But she did love him. And she would love him tomorrow. She would love his lists and his systems and plans. She would love his spotless truck cab and his annoying insistence on drinking only water.

Someone kneeled next to her, grabbing the towel she was using and replacing it with a clean, damp one. Warm, brown eyes met hers under the table and she melted, once again, into a pile of ooze. At the sight of Lance, always willing to help, her heart puddled in her chest like spilled orange juice on the refinished wood floors. And there, on her knees wiping up the last drops of spilled juice, Daisy accepted the fact that maybe loving Lance Matthew wasn't so terrifying after all.

AFTER BREAKFAST, when the Porters had left for their hiking trip, Lance was lounging on the wicker sofa in the sunroom with a book, when Daisy knocked lightly on the door frame. Happy to be interrupted, he sat up and dog-eared the page with a flourish before closing the book.

Daisy raised her eyebrow at him, "Need a bookmark?"

He gave her a wink, "Nope. I've turned over a new leaf."

"Oh yeah?" She stepped closer, and his heart hammered.

Lance swallowed heavily. This was it, wasn't it? He wiped his suddenly sweaty palms on his jeans. "Mmm-hmm. Someone I love very much told me I need to loosen up." Daisy took another step toward him and he stood.

Daisy covered her mouth, embarrassed. "Did I really?" They were close now, only a few inches between them. "I'm sorry, Lance—"

"Don't be, my love." Lance brushed a wayward strand of hair behind her ear again. "You were right."

She shook her head, but he continued. He needed to tell her what she'd taught him.

"You were right. I was... I am," he corrected, "inflexible. I'm stubborn and probably boring. But Daisy, you—" Lance prayed for the words to explain adequately. "You are life and joy and spirit. The way you grab hold of moments makes me want to do the same. Every day I spend with you is better for your presence."

Daisy sniffed and closed her eyes, moisture brimming at the edges. Lance placed his hands on her upper arms and ducked his head to look in her eyes. "You are amazing. You are stubborn, too," she choked out a laugh through her running nose, "but I would rather fight with you than live in perfect harmony with someone else."

"Daisy, can we try again? I've been asking God for an answer since I booked this reservation, and He hasn't given me the big, fat yes I was looking for. And now, every time we get close to talking, something interrupts us." He glanced at the door, "I keep expecting Bonnie to barge through the doors demanding your attention." He waited, but the rest of the house was silent. "But He hasn't said no, either. Which is why I came."

"Is that why you left dirty clothes out in your room? Or intentionally put your water on the table instead of the coaster?" her smile was growing and she continued. "Or why you dripped sauce on your shirt? Just to prove you could do it?"

Lance ducked his head. Apparently, he wasn't as sneaky as he thought. "I just thought if I could show you that I wasn't the uptight, obsessive man you thought I was, maybe you would give me another chance."

Daisy just laughed and stepped closer, wrapping her arms around his waist. "Lance Matthews, I never want you to be something you aren't." She tipped her head, "You know, since you left, I started making my own lists?" His eyebrows shot skyward in disbelief. "It's true. I'm a certified list-maker now."

"Sounds dangerous," Lance joked.

"All I'm saying is, I think maybe we balance each other out more than we thought."

Lance nodded, looking down at the woman he loved. "I'm better when I'm with you."

"Same," she said, and his heart raced.

Lance cleared his throat and said the words he hadn't actually said to her yet, "I love you."

Daisy's arms tightened around his waist and she grinned up at him. "And I love you." Unable to resist, Lance lowered his mouth to hers, pulling her into his arms and deepening the kiss until the space between them seemed to disappear entirely. The house could have come crashing down around them and Lance would have been completely unconcerned, as long as his lips remained locked to hers. The kiss was sweet and hot, hinting at the future of things to come.

"Daisy Bloom, I choose to love you every day."

"Sixty years of every days," Daisy responded with a smile.

"An eternity of every days," he replied, before lowering his lips to hers again. It was the promise of forever, made with open eyes and a soaring heart—and sealed with a kiss.

EPILOGUE

*I*t had been more than three months, and while her beloved husband had made incredible strides towards recovery, Laura Bloom knew her life would never be the same. She stood in the kitchen and waited for her coffee to brew, like she had every morning since Keith had his stroke. Before that life-changing Thanksgiving Day, her wonderful husband had brought her a cup in bed each morning.

Their family had come together since the stroke. And it seemed like they would be adding to the family soon. Hawthorne had shared his plans to propose to Avery, and Daisy had brought Lance to brunch last week.

Laura smiled, thinking of her free-spirited

daughter. What a joy it had been in the last few months to watch Daisy step into the role of business owner. Daisy had been so heartbroken when she returned from New York, Laura had prayed every day for Daisy to bloom where God had planted her.

Lance brought the perfect balance of steadiness to Daisy's tendency to drift. He was an answer to years of prayers Laura had laid before her Creator, just like she did for each of her children.

Her thoughts shifted to the others. There was something going on with Poppy, but Laura didn't know what it was. Admittedly, she'd been preoccupied with Keith; so many opportunities she usually had to connect with her children had been missed because of rehab appointments and puzzles with her husband.

Laura said a quick prayer for Poppy and whatever secrets she was keeping. Hopefully, Poppy would lean into the support of her family. No matter what was going on, the Bloom Family was committed to loving the way God did—unconditionally.

ABOUT POPPY'S PROPOSAL

BOOK 2 IN THE BLOOM SISTERS SERIES

She vowed he would never hurt her again.
He hides his pain behind a campaign smile.

Harrison Coulter is in the spotlight. Rumored to be the next candidate for governor, there is just one problem – the people won't elect the most eligible bachelor to the state's highest office. He needs a wife, but he isn't looking for love. There *is* one woman from his past though...

Poppy Bloom has roots as deep as the produce she grows on Bloom's Farm. When her livelihood is threatened and she finds herself helpless to make a difference, Poppy agrees to a proposal she never saw coming.

Old feelings blossom into something new, but

their individual goals clash with the promises made to each other. How will God use this marriage that was strategized instead of starry-eyed to open them both to the power of love?

Find out in Poppy's Proposal, Book 2 of The Bloom Sisters Series.

GIVING BACK

One of my favorite privileges as an author is the ability to honor those from real life in the pages of my fictional stories. Occasionally, I contribute this gift to a charity auction, as I did with a character from Daisy's story to benefit Project Hope (pjhope.org), an organization based in Missouri "To give HOPE locally and around the world by presenting the gospel of Jesus through relational ministry." If you would like to learn more about the wonderful mission of Project Hope, please visit their website.

Jacquie Dowdy is more than the fictional family friend and godmother figure in Daisy's story. Her friends chose to honor Jacquie within the pages of my books, and I could not have been more thrilled, because she also happens to be a woman I admire a great deal. From the beginning, Jacquie has been one of my biggest supporters. I am blessed to know her, and her testimony impacted me much as it did Daisy in the book.

In the process of preparing to write Jacquie into this book, I researched more about her story of faithfulness in the midst of opposition. Without sharing specifics, I hope I did her character and her story justice. Although Jacquie did retire as CEO after working her way up within a hotel empire, her biggest joys in life are Jesus and her grandchildren, whom she loves fiercely. Thank you for your example and your friendship, Jacquie.

NOTE TO READERS

Thank you for picking up (or downloading!) this book. As any author can tell you, reviews are incredibly important to our success. Please, please, please take a minute to leave a review.

Daisy and Lance were a blast to write. Not just because Daisy might be based loosely on a certain scatter-brained author and Lance on her Type A husband.

I love how these characters found balance in each other, recognizing that perfection is impossible and grace is essential. Mr. Higgins's sage advice about choosing love every day until any other choice seems impossible is a reminder I often give myself. I pray my books encourage you in your faith and through your struggles, whatever they may be.

You can learn more about my upcoming projects at my website: www.taragraceericson.com or by signing up for my newsletter. Just for signing up, you will get a free story!

If you've never read my other books, I'd love for you to read the Main Street Minden Series and dive into the world of Minden, Indiana. Or, read more about the Bloom Family in Hoping for Hawthorne.

Thank you again for all your support and encouragement.

ACKNOWLEDGMENTS

First and foremost, to my Jehovah-Jireh. You provide these words, even when I think I have none left. You provide the time to write them, even when I am convinced there is none left. And you have given me a life of abundance in Jesus Christ. May yours be the Glory.

To my editor, Jessica from BH Writing Services. I adore you. Thank you for loving my crazy, pinpointing how to make it better, and overall being a bright spot in my days of this stay-at-home-order.

To Gabbi, always a steadying influence and a godly inspiration. Call me more often, friend.

To Hannah Jo Abbott and Mandi Blake, my writing besties. Thank you for the random chats, the accountability, the cheerleading, and the writing sprints. For a writer, I find myself at a loss for words to share how important you are to me.

To my parents, who showed me true love and God's grace. I love you.

To the women of Fellowship Bible Church and our devoted group, thank you for your prayers and your support. Coming into your group two years ago felt like coming home.

Thank you to all my readers, without whose support and encouragement, I would have given up a long time ago.

And finally, to my husband. It's not easy to be married to a writer, especially one on a deadline. I've never really based a hero on you before, but Lance comes close. My love for you is overwhelming. I am the luckiest woman in the world because you've chosen to love me for an eternity of every days. Mr. B and Little C; keep telling Mommy stories. You are my sunshine.

ABOUT THE AUTHOR

Tara Grace Ericson lives in Missouri with her husband and two sons. She studied engineering and worked as an engineer for many years before embracing her creative side to become a full-time author. Her first book, Falling on Main Street, was written mostly from airport waiting areas and bleak hotel rooms as she traveled in her position as a sales engineer.

She loves cooking, crocheting, and reading books by the dozen. Her writing partner is usually her black lab - Ruby - and a good cup of coffee or tea. Tara unashamedly watches Hallmark movies all winter long, even though they are predictable and cheesy. She loves a good "happily ever after" with an engaging love story. That's why Tara focuses on writing clean contemporary romance, with an emphasis on Christian faith and living. She wants to encourage her readers with stories of men and women who live out their faith in tough situations.

BOOKS BY TARA GRACE ERICSON

The Main Street Minden Series

Falling on Main Street

Winter Wishes

Spring Fever

Summer to Remember

Kissing in the Kitchen: A Main Street Minden Novella

The Bloom Sisters Series

Hoping for Hawthorne - A Bloom Family Novella

A Date for Daisy

Made in the USA
Las Vegas, NV
22 February 2022

44401052R00184